T0137659

Bet Sharrukin

Bet Sharrukin

The Son of Perdition

Allen Bonck

iUniverse®

BET SHARRUKIN
THE SON OF PERDITION

iUniverse books may be ordered through booksellers or by contacting:

iUniverse
1663 Liberty Drive
Bloomington, IN 47403
www.iuniverse.com
1-800-Authors (1-800-288-4677)

ISBN: 978-1-5320-8589-5 (sc)
ISBN: 978-1-5320-8588-8 (hc)
ISBN: 978-1-5320-8587-1 (e)

Library of Congress Control Number: 2019918665

Print information available on the last page.

iUniverse rev. date: 11/20/2019

Artist conception of an Ophan angel [as seen on the front cover]. Ophans are seen in the book of Ezekiel, and described as a wheel within a wheel.

DEDICATION

To my wife Linda, who has persistently encouraged me to write a prophetic fictional story using sound prophetic truths.

CONTENTS

CHAPTER ONE

The Call

In 1962 in the small town of Ermia, Iran, an historic enclave of the ancient Assyrian people. [1] A wrinkled hand reached out to a 1950s model radio. It turned the knob, and the voice of the Shah of Iran crackled out. [2]

"I require this and this alone. Believe me! Believe in me! I will give you the Persian Empire again and it will be glorious!"

The crowd's enthusiastic cheer poured out from the speakers and filled out an under-furnished Middle Eastern living room, where an old man in his sixties sat in a worn out arm chair. A tattered book dangled in his hand.

A small ten year old boy sprawled by the old man's feet. The boy was persistent in erasing a misspelled Farsi word from his lesson sheet. Suddenly, the old man's book reached impact across the room, smashing into a small devotional altar for Jesus. The young boy looked up at the old man. The old man only stared back. He uncoiled on the armchair and put his face in his hands. The boy gingerly approached his Grandfather.

"Do you need your high blood medicine?" asked the boy.

"No Pul, [pronounced Paul] just bring me back the book." answered the old man.

Pul obeyed. The book had plummeted on the altar. As he re-organized the flowers, and candles, Pul wondered about what the Shah said.

"Was that man lying?" Pul asked as he placed the image of Christ back in its rightful place.

Grandfather responded, "He has no place to speak about an empire."

"Isn't he the Shah? Shouldn't he know?" Pul asked again intensely.

Pul handed the book back to his grandfather. But stayed outside his orbit. The old man scanned through the pages expertly. Then, he revealed before the boy, a captivating illustration.

"This is the royal palace of Dur-Sharrukin, and it was opulent and profusely adorned by engraved reliefs." the old man explained. [3]

The boy's attention landed on the images that came alive. A winged bull with the bust of a king, then onto the eagle-faced Seraphim, and to the swirling tree of life, then on a powerful Assyrian god encircled in flames, tensing his great arrow over an intimidated army.[4] All of it grabbed at Pul and a great battle unfolded before him. In his imagination, he saw swords clash, heard the cries of war, and the thunderous gallops. Then, the sand settled. An Assyrian's head in the grips of the Babylonian enemy. The Babylonians prevailed.

Pul was shown another page of the book. A painting of a king, in his grasp was the visage of Christ printed on a scroll. Abgar, the first Christian Assyrian king. It was this king who converted to Christianity in the first century A.D. and ushered in the second Assyrian golden age. Nearly, all his people followed his example and even today nearly all Assyrians are Christians.

"Pul..." the old man said. "It is fortunate that we have the hope of eternal life through Christ."

"But?" Pul questioned.

"Because Pul, true Christians make lousy empire builders." added the old man.

"Why?" Pul asked.

"Because Christians are supposed to look for an empire whose builder and maker is God, not one built by themselves." the old man answered. [5]

Pul asked, "The Shah is a fool, then?"

Grandfather responded, "No, he is right. But, it will be Assyria that shall be a nation and empire again."

Assyria? Pul thought to himself. He hasn't heard that name in a long time. He looked at his grandfather, unbelieving.

"Pul recite Isaiah 19:23 for me." requested the old man.

"Uh...um..." stammered Pul.

He turned quiet and felt the weight of his grandfather's judgmental stare.

The old man relented, "There will be a road from Egypt to Assyria at the end of this age."[6] He continued in a more serious tone, "The scriptures may mean nothing to you now, but it meant everything to us back then."

Pul knew what he meant. He held his head down but his eyes instinctively came up to the huge slashed scar on the old man's neck.

"They tried to kill us in an attempted genocide, they betrayed us by giving our land to others, with nothing left to call our own. But we will not always be the victims." added the old man.

The boy looked up at his grandfather who was now charged with hope.

"Pul, after the genocide, your father and I could only just rebuild and stabilize our lives, survive. But you and your generation need to have the vision and strength to make it happen... restore Assyria!" exclaimed the old man.

The boy tried to find something to say but comes short. The old man's mood shifted upward and he laughed.

"Pul, you can go outside now." He said.

Pul cracked the door open, he clearly heard his grandfather say.

"All battles are won in the spirit realm, never forget this."

The boy shut the door behind him and he was greeted by the high noon light. He started to walk and his grandfather's words weighed heavier with his every step. *What now?* Pul thought to himself. His feet took him next door to an unfinished home of brick and clay. It is where his friend, Marodeen lives. Marodeen's family was not any better off than Pul's. Pul perched on an open window with a bright blue painted frame.

"Pst! psssst, Marodeen" whispered Pul.

Marodeen who shared the same age as Pul but is bigger, set down the knife and veggies he was cutting and turned to see Pul.

"Thank the heavens!" exclaimed Marodeen as he bolted past Pul through the window and leaving his chores.

Pul tried to catch up. They raced past modest houses and a hectic market at its peak. An angry mother's yell was heard from the distance. Whatever breath Marodeen still has was spent on laughter.

"Your mother's going to kill me." said Pul.

"So, what? Chopping onions will be the death of me." Marodeen laughed.

The boys splashed down on a grassy patch with a grand sky above. They're both quiet as they ponder.

"Pul... what's got you?" Marodeen curiously asked.

"What do you mean?" Pul asked back.

"You're always bad at hiding it. Did they gang up on you again?"

"No, Marodeen it's not them... It's just that my grandfather told me the strangest thing today." Pul sat up and looked off somewhere.

"I think I know what he said..." Marodeen said as he sat up with him.

"You do? Mister Know-it-all." Pul knew how Marodeen hated being called that.

"Don't call me that!"

Pul finally cracked a smile, and the tension passed.

"Did your grandfather talk about restoring Assyria?" Marodeen asked.

"I can't believe it! How did you know?" Pul asked in surprise.

"Actually my father told me the same thing two weeks ago."

"What do you think it all means, what do we do?" Pul asked.

"Stop talking and listen for a minute. I've had some time to think about this and I believe it's about spiritual warfare. I think, I know where to go for answers. Come on Pul, come with me." Marodeen said excitedly.

He ran off with Pul in tow, coming to the Assyrian Church near their homes.

They slowed down and entered the church.

A priest, Father Youkhana, the head of the local church. He was an older man, quick-witted and his beard was nearly gray. But the old priest still stood as straight as an arrow. He was in deep prayer on the front pew. The two boys knelt beside him and made the instinctive sign of the cross.

Marodeen whispered, "Father Youkhana? Father...?"

"I'm in the middle of a conversation, Marodeen." The priest responded seriously.

"But Father, we need your help... you see..." Marodeen explained but was cut short by Pul.

"Do you know about spiritual warfare?"

The priest flinched. Now, they have his attention.

"Why do you need to fight in the spirit?" the priest asked.

"We want to establish a new Assyria...Can you help?" Pul asked as he looked intently at the priest.

"That's a dangerous thing, you're talking about breaking down existing borders, setting up new governments. Boys like you should be out playing." The priest said.

"We can't do that, Father, we've been called..." exclaimed Pul.

Marodeen chimed in, "We need to learn what we have to know."

Father Youkhana finished his prayers and sat down on the pew. "If you really want to learn, then learn this. The church is the only Assyrian institution remaining intact after the genocide. There are no political parties or paramilitary groups for you to join..."

Pul interrupted, "Then we'll make our own group."

"Yeah, we'll make our own." echoed Marodeen.

The priest was slightly frustrated. "Boys, boys, aren't you being overzealous?"

"Father, we have to do this, our families are counting on us. We can't shake it." insisted Pul.

The priest stood up and said, "The Muslims in charge of Iran will not tolerate a Christian restoration of Assyria. As far as they are concerned, Assyria is dead and gone. Only Islam matters now... and the land is theirs." explained the priest before he left the two boys.

CHAPTER TWO

Contact

1968, in a field behind the church, seven cautious young men seemed to appear from nowhere. They huddled around the huge tree by the back border and at the center are sixteen years old, Pul and Marodeen.

Marodeen spoke up, "All right boys, we don't have much time. Where's the new recruit?"

An older teenager from the group stepped forward.

"Welcome brother. I am Marodeen and this is Pul." Marodeen offered the older teenager a welcoming hand.

The recruit received Marodeen's hand and acknowledged Pul. Pul was smaller than the others but was the most formidable. [7]

"Welcome, you are in the midst of a growing group of Assyrian men who wish to form a union to represent the Assyrian cause." Pul began.

"Thank you for asking me..." said the new recruit but he does not look at Pul in the eye.

"Is something wrong?" asked Pul.

"Well, if you don't mind, may I ask why we're meeting at the church? I would assume the church wouldn't react kindly to hosting nationalists?" answered the recruit.

"We're not exactly sanctioned... We're working behind the scenes, and to be clear, we see ourselves as a simple union organization that puts forth Assyrian views in public discourse." Marodeen responded.

"In short, to become a part of the government in Iran." Pul added.

All the boys began chuckling. As the meeting continued... Father Youkhana looked from the rear door of the church. A young priest came up behind him and looked at the group of young men.

"Do you want me to break up those misfits, father?" the younger priest asked Father Youkhana.

"No, they're still part of our church, and their families are good people. We do not endorse their actions because it could bring another wave of persecution on us if the Muslims were to feel offended or threatened. This concern is not unwarranted, don't you agree?" Father Youkhana said.

"Yes." The young priest replied, nodding his head.

"So let's pray they don't get too zealous." Father Youkhana said as he put his hands up and walked away.

The young priest shifted his attention back to Pul. The group noticed. They dispersed and walked away discretely.

A few weeks later, Pul was at a communion service. Bells tolled and the service was over. Pul was leaving through the rear of the sanctuary. Suddenly, he heard someone beckoned to him from the corridor. It's the young priest, he went over to Pul apprehensively.

"It is time for you to make contact Pul." said the young priest.

"Pardon me Father, but with who?" Pul asked confused.

"Make an appointment with Father Ibrahim." The young priest added.

"Father, have I done something to get in trouble?" Pul asked with apprehension.

The priest continued, "You cannot tell anyone about this conversation or about the appointment to come. Do you understand? No one.". The priest left Pul nodding and wide-eyed.

A week later, Pul still in his school clothes, went to the monastery. The priest motioned for Pul to follow him through the stone corridors, deep into the building, like an ominous apparition. There were no windows and no other sounds except their footsteps. They entered a room, the priest directed him to sit on a chair with a small table in front of it. There were eight Monks wearing hoods seated just inside the back of the room against the walls. There were four on each side of the room, further in the room was the altar table.

Father Ibrahim, a young priest not much older than Pul, was directly on the other side of the table, facing Pul. He was the ninth and the only one without his hood on.

Father Ibrahim nervously began, "What I am about to tell you must never be revealed to anyone outside this room." He continued, "The heart of the matter is that not all the priests in the Assyrian church are opposed to the new Assyria." He paused. "This is because they are not Christians at all... We are priests that are under authority and oath to the old Assyrian god named Asshur." Father Ibrahim spoke as though this god has actually been talking with him. He continued, "Asshur is very much interested in restoring Assyria. He desires to put all his power and influence into seeing it done."

Pul tried to keep a mocking smirk from forming. He re-composed himself, and asked, "Just how would I get this support? How would it come?"

Father Ibrahim simply put his finger on his lips. This shushed Pul. "Look down and don't say anything." The father put his hood over his head and looked straight down.

A great flash of light. Two beings appeared next to Pul. One on each side. These entities were at least seven feet tall with three sets of wings. Their faces were like eagles, with large-feathered combs on their heads, looking like Roman centurion helmets. [8] Without a word, they reached out and touched Pul's shoulders. His whole body trembled and paralyzed where he was.

A second, even brighter light engulfed the room. Another supernatural being appeared, towering behind Father Ibrahim. Pul saw that Father Ibrahim shook through his robe, terrified. Pul thought what he was seeing was an angel. He was larger and had only two wings but they stretched across the room. From the waist down, he was covered with feathers that were brightly-colored like a peacock's and looked luminescent.

It took a moment for Pul to realize that the angel levitated above the floor, suspended in front of a large wheel of fire. The wheel moved and rotated as though it was alive. It was actually alive. [9]

The angel spoke to Pul directly in perfect Aramaic, the ancient language of Assyria.

The angel said, "Sharrukinbanipal, I have come for you..."

Pul wanted to speak but doesn't.

"I am Asshur, the chief god of Assyria, from time and the beginning."

Pul wanted to speak but, felt a little pressure from the Angels on his shoulders.

"I have chosen you. You will lead the Assyrian people back into their land, Sharrukinbanipal." Asshur continued.

Paul whispered, "Sharrukinbanipal?" He noticed Father Ibrahim flinched.

Asshur snapped at Pul. "Silence! You don't know what your name means... Do you?"

Pul said nothing. "Very smart, you can learn. Bet Sharrukin means, The son of the legitimate king. From this point on, you will answer to that name when I call. I will make you the legitimate king, and you will be a son to me."

Pul mouths to himself, "A king?"

Asshur continued "You must never question my directions, my timing or requests. You must be obedient without reservation of mind, quick to act when needed, and patient to sit when told. I will choose your friends and your enemies. I will also give you full access to intelligence gathered by my ministers. I will fight every battle in the spirit before you will engage the enemy. Father Ibrahim is your mentor and will represent me. You can trust him, do what he says."

As fast as they had appeared, the group of spiritual beings disappeared. They left the room so dark that Pul scarcely saw his hand in front of his face. As his eyes began to adjust, he saw that the hooded monks were all around him on their knees giving him their obeisance.

Pul shocked. "What are you doing? Stop it!"

"Do you not know who you are? You are the son of Asshur, the son of god, Bet Sharrukin." Father Ibrahim replied.

"Do I have a choice?" Pul responded. Then he realized that he had not been asked anything, but rather told everything.

"Will you really say, No?" Father Ibrahim asked.

There was silence in the room, finally Pul said, "I guess we have work to do..."

Pul tossed and turned in bed that night. Asshur's presence and words lingered in his mind. He got out of bed, it took him a moment to compose himself and he sighed. He sat at his desk and grabbed a pen and a tattered notebook from the drawer.

He wrote, "I can still see this vision with my eyes awake, every detail precise and complete. If this was a dream, the power of my mind and imagination is far greater than I ever thought. My mind is racing one hundred miles an hour. But still

I could never share this with anyone." He set the pen down and pondered at how ridiculous it all seemed. He ripped out the page he just wrote on, crumpled it and threw it away.

That next Sunday, Pul went to church with his family and as he came in through the door, he looked up to see a row of monks and priests in an alcove on his left side. He looked at them and they made eye contact. Very discreetly, they closed their eyes and bowed their heads in unison. Pul's knees went weak. He stumbled and nearly passed out. From that moment, he knew that it had all been real. The contact, the call, were real.

CHAPTER THREE

Pul's Training

Father Ibrahim and Pul are sitting ona bench in the churches small garden.

"Pul, you are Asshur's tool to build his empire. As you are now, you're far from being worthy of this endeavor. Your success will be Assyria's success."

"Then what do I need to do, Father?"

A boy around Pul's age passed by the church on a bicycle. Father Ibrahim noticed Pul grimacing.

"That boy... He's a Shiite correct?" Father Ibrahim inquired.

"I think so... He used to pick on me and Marodeen when we were younger. I don't think he still remembers me though."

"Pul, it's time for you to start disarming them. Understand your enemy, you must learn to communicate with everyone not just your friends."

"What are you getting at, Father?"

Suddenly, a gust of wind blew. Pul heard a crash and ran out of the court yard. Further up the cobblestone road, the boy and his bicycle are laid out on the ground, near a large tree branch. Pul turned to see what Father Ibrahim might have to say. But he's nowhere in sight. Pul ran to the boy and helped him up.

"Don't touch me!" grunted the boy. He did not appreciate Pul's help.

Pul ignored the rebuff and asked, "What happened? Are you all right?"

"It just fell on me from nowhere." The boy relented as he brushed the dust off his clothes.

Pul inspected the bicycle. "The chain is off the ring." Pul said.

The boy retorted, "Well, fix it..."

Pul looked back at the boy and remembered the lessons he was supposed to learn, especially when it comes to controlling his anger.

Under the shade of a nearby tree, the boy unrolled a mat. Then he started kneeling and reciting prayers. Pul brought the bike under the tree and tried to re-attach the chain to the ring but his eyes shifted frequently to the boy in supplication. Pul accomplished his task in fixing the bike. He sat beside the boy and waited, now they engaged in conversation. The boy explained something and Pul listened intently.

"I see, I see. It's no wonder that the Muslims are in charge of the country..." Pul agreed.

The boy has a satisfied look.

"Can you teach me more? I know I'm just an Assyrian, but I really want to know." asked Pul.

The boy invited Pul to meet some of his friends. Pul made a mental note that, *flattery is better than confrontation.* He learned his lesson. [10]

A few weeks later, Marodeen and another union member were walking down town. They stopped in their tracks when they saw Pul mingling with Shiite boys who were sporting nice suits and fashionable pompadours loitering outside a store downtown.

The union member muttered under his breath, "Please tell me this isn't real."

Marodeen quickly shared a glance with Pul, who continued in conversation with the Shiites. "C'mon let's go." Marodeen whispered.

"What do you mean C'mon?"

As Marodeen walked away, the union member followed.

Sometimes it's hard for the Assyrian nationalists to understand why Pul was friendly with the enemy. But Pul knew his reasons as to why. He was making headway for future relationships.

Father Ibrahim began to intensify Pul's training. In a deep location within the monastery, Pul was sitting at a table with Father Ibrahim.

"Visualize yourself outside this monastery… Imagine your most favorite location in the world… The place you feel the safest." ordered Father Ibrahim.

"It's been an hour, Father. What if trances don't work on me?" asked Pul.

"Time is a requirement! Now, multiply your imagination with vividness… This will become your reality. Focus!" the priest quipped.

From the darkness, Pul slowly manifested inside a hazy impression of his living room from his childhood. He sat in a chair with his eyes closed and his palms flat on his lap.

Father Ibrahim insisted, "Come on, truly see every detail…"

The room became more vivid and real. Pul opened his eyes. The 1950s radio, and the altar in front of him. He realized he's sitting on his grandfather's chair.

"I can't believe it… I'm home." Pul marveled. A genuine happiness in his voice.

"Is this room fit for a king?" inquired the priest.

"No it's not".

"Then let's make it bigger." commanded the priest. With the priest's help, Pul made the walls move back and the ceiling rose up. They made floors and columns of marble.

"Is your chair fit for a king?" the priest asked.

"No."

"Then let's fix it too."

They built a throne for Pul to sit on.

"Do you like your room?" asked the priest.

"Yes."

"Look behind your throne." ordered the priest.

Pul looked and found a door. He opened it only to find another room. This one looked like a high-end executive office with only the best furniture, lighting, carpet and more.

Father Ibrahim said, "This is yours, Pul. It's your office… Do you like it?"

Pul explored the room like a child. "Yes, I do!"

"You can change it any way you desire or just enjoy it. This is your spirit office, your new special place." added the priest.

Pul and Father Ibrahim continued going to Pul's throne room and office whenever they hold spirit classes. Then during one session, they came into the throne room and Pul saw three new doors at the rear of the room. One double door at the center of the rear wall, and one single wide door in each rear corner.

"Would you like to go through the center door." asked the priest.

"Sure."

They walked through the door. Pul tried to process all the splendor of the room. It's a throne room but far more elegant than his. A Seraphim on the throne and an Ophanim, a wheel of fire, directly behind him. These looked very similar to Asshur's consorts from Pul's original encounter. The room itself had a myriad of spirits and lesser angels. They all seemed to focus on Pul.

Pul got this feeling that he was underdressed for a banquet and started to feel totally out of place. As he stood in front of the angels, Pul began to bow but a pair of hands held him in place.

"No! Stand up straight, look him in the eye. Don't blink. Don't talk." The priest whispered.

"You don't look that special." said the Seraphim.

Pul didn't respond or blink his eyes. Instead, he stared at the angel for what seemed like forever. Finally, the angel bowed his head.

"How can I help you?" asked the angel.

Father Ibrahim answered, "Mighty Baraquel... Seraphim of the first order, I..."

"Shut up, priest! I did not address you!" shouted the angel.

Pul's anger flashed, and he shouted back with indignation. "What's your name?! How long have you held this position? Do you want to keep it?"

At this time, the Seraphim and everyone else in the room fell prostrate before Pul. Not a word was spoken.

Father Ibrahim was amazed at the authority that Pul had with the angels and spirits. It was somewhat unsettling to him. The priest pointed Pul to a large door on the right of the room and opened it. He began to go through but stopped halfway. He stepped back and allowed Pul to go through first. They left the throne room.

There was a long hallway in front of them. It was illuminated by itself. No actual source can be found. It was large enough that it could accommodate a large angel. They followed the hallway.

"We are now travelling between nodes on the Assyrian tree of life."[11] The priest said as they moved along.

He opened his palms and presented a miniature tree of life for Pul to see. A sort of three dimensional translucent hologram, which was floating above the priests hands. Pul observed it closely, but it didn't look particularly like a tree but a series of leafy rosettes, arranged and constructed in a strange connected lattice pattern.

"The throne room we were just in is only one of the nodes in the tree, there are actually many thrones. And there are many levels within each node." The priest continued.

The tour continued, they passed through a series of throne rooms. Each room, or node was somewhat different, the angels and spirits were different. However, they all graciously greeted and bowed before Pul as he passed. It seemed that news moved quickly in the tree of life. As soon as Pul left a node, those in the node showed signs of fear for Pul and his priest.

"The spirits and angels here have special talents and understanding of different subjects and needs. They are all here to serve you." Father Ibrahim explained. He placed his hand on Pul's shoulder and turned him around. He looked at him in the eye and said, "Never allow yourself to be mentally lazy. If you lose track of reality...the next step is insanity."

CHAPTER FOUR

Pul's Rise

Pul in his 20's, was in the middle of an impassioned speech in front of the newly formed official Assyrian Union. The men were engaged with his every word. Just outside our sense of reality, Pul's spirit helpers and counselors were just as impressed. He was making great progress.

Pul was in the garden behind the church in Ermia. He had been given unofficial permission to use the facilities as needed. He and a younger Assyrian assistant went over agendas and strategies. Marodeen approached him with drinks in his hand. He was in his hospital doctor uniform.

Pul was always glad to see his old friend. "I can always count on you to be early. Are your chores all done? Your mom isn't going to kill me, right?" Pul said with a smile on his face.

"It has been a while." laughed Marodeen.

Paul discreetly dismissed the assistant. "We'll finish this in the morning." The assistant left quietly.

Marodeen handed Pul the drink and asked, "You've been having dinner with Shiites? I've only been gone a while."

"Are you angry?" questioned Pul.

"No, no. You know me, I wouldn't be here if I was." Marodeen remarked.

Pul sat up straight and looked at Marodeen. "I know that many people are very concerned about my Shiite friends, but I believe it is needful if we're to meet our goals."

Marodeen's countenance dropped. "I was on duty yesterday when a man was rushed to the E.R. We looked through his case, and found he was beaten by a group of Shiites, simply because he had a cross pendant on his neck. His face had been beaten badly, beyond recognition. I cried for him, Pul." said Marodeen.

Pul responded, "I really believe in my heart that I'm leading us in the right direction. You don't have to worry about me."

Marodeen sighed, "Just so you'll know, I still support our cause."

Pul held up his drink and they toasted. "To the new Assyria."

At the Assyrian Union Office in Tehran, 1979. The phone rang to no end. Pul, now 27, perched on the balcony with several other men. They're craning to watch a huge street protest below. Someone finally picked up the phone and handed it to Pul. Pul responded to the caller, "It seems like everyone in our network has called me in the last hour. What do you have for me?" He asked and stepped out of the crowd.

The caller, a Union officer responded, "Evidently the fundamentalist Shiites in Iran have been plotting the Shah's overthrow for quite some time. The Shah's demise is near."

Pul just smiled as he had known all of this for some time, from his spirit sources.

The officer anxiously continued. "What will our move be?"

"We will remain neutral. Mitigate the chance of reprisals from whoever wins the battle. Whatever happens will be a mixed bag for... us..." responded Pul.

The noise of protesters being roughed up by the police below distracted Pul from the phone, which is accidently disconnected.

The next day, Pul is in his union office with Father Ibrahim. The sun drenched Pul, who stood by the window.

Father Ibrahim commented, "You seem amused." the priest walked to the window.

Pul smiled. "I just realized that no country is too big to fall."

The spirits in the room smiled at each other while just outside, a Coca-Cola billboard was torn down by the protesters.

Pul prepared himself for meeting with the Assyrian Union members. He opened the doors of the conference room in a rush. The room was hushed and grim. A meager crowd of members greeted him.

"Where are the others?" Pul asked.

A union member answered "The rest have left the country with their families, when the borders were still open. We all want to leave as well."

Pul stepped up. "Don't fear these Islamic state revolutionaries! We're 100,000 people strong. We can wade through this."

One of the union members piped up. "This new Iranian government is already closing down our Farsi speaking churches. We all know that the Muslims have a history of killing Assyrians, anytime there's a change in government. In Muslim nations the minorities suffer, Christians and Jews at the top of the list."

Another member stepped forward. "The country is choking under Sharia Law.

Those who run will be better off than the ones who stay." Most of them left.

Pul continued to work with his Shiite friends and a new government developed. This new government accommodated Iran's minorities by allowing five seats in the Parliament for their own elected representatives. [12]

Pul and Father Ibrahim just smiled when they heard the news.

"Surely one of these seats is mine." Pul said and laughed with Father Ibrahim.

Pul eventually got elected to represent the Assyrians in the government. The position was mostly symbolic but with Pul's spiritual talents, he made the most of the opportunity. He was able to hob nob with Shiites at the highest levels. He was able to get an opportunity to speak in front of the entire Parliament general assembly. It went well and Pul was allowed to represent Iran in many diplomatic events, even outside Iran. He, of course was pressing for his Assyrian restoration. He felt that he must separate the Assyrians from their Christian heritage, as in the West. They had been perceived by the Shiites as enemies. He must convince them that the Assyrians are a different kind of Christian, the kind that does not pose a threat to Islam.

The Assyrian Union has become an international organization with chapters all over the world. They are trying to unify and coordinate Assyrians into a cohesive people. Pul became the head of the international union and moved his main focus to Iraq. Iraq was the main homeland for the Assyrian nation and if the Assyrians were to have a new nation it will probably be in northern Iraq.

Iraq, under the leadership of Saddam Hussein, challenged the United States in a confrontation in Kuwait. The outcome was a new government in Iraq, with a new constitution. This new constitution provided for Iraqi minorities to receive their own autonomous provinces within Iraq, if approved by the Iraqi government. The Kurds of northern Iraq were the first minority in Iraq to receive a province. This was not surprising since the Kurds are Muslims and not a threat to Islam.

The Iraqi Assyrian union began to reach out to the international community. This appeared to be helpful and early in 2015, they received an approval from the Iraqi government to have their own province, the process began. None of this was reported in the international press, who saw this as an internal Iraqi issue.

But the implications were not missed by the other Muslims in the Middle East.

Pul was in his union office in Tehran. An organized mess of people and boxes shuttled to and from the office. Pul and his team were celebrating with wine amidst the hectic work going on around them. But, within days, Pul still in his Tehran offices was preparing his people to leave when the news was heard from Iraq, that a group of Islamic fighters called ISIS have attacked the Iraqi towns of Fallujah and Ramadi. They quickly defeated the Iraqi security forces and moved to Mosul. Pul and Father Ibrahim with others listen to a radio report.

"Sunni Muslims that were fighting in Syria suddenly attacked Iraq. Damage is focused on Mosul which is to be the capital of the new Assyria. Within days, the city has fallen to ISIS. The Kurdish militias have fled the area in a total retreat. The international community begins to gather together to keep ISIS from establishing a Caliphate in the greater Middle East." The radio reporter announced.

Reports came to Pul through the Iraqi Assyrian union that the primary targets of ISIS were the Assyrians and other minorities in Mosul. The motives of Isis was to kill the new Assyrian state before it gets formed. It also became apparent that the Iraqi military would not stand and fight to protect the Assyrians. It had only taken fifteen hundred ISIS fighters to chase off thirty thousand Iraqi soldiers.

Pul and Father Ibrahim went to Asshur to get answers. They requested an audience with Asshur and was able to see him in Pul's spirit office. Father Ibrahim was included in the session. Pul was incensed about the setback.

"Don't you have any influence with Isis? Why are they allowed to kill Assyrians?" Pul asked angrily.

Asshur heard Pul and calmly responded, "Any real progress always requires blood. The international community hasn't responded with compassion for your cause. They cannot be touched just by your pleas. They now know who you are, and they see your suffering. Public opinion will support your cause. This was not the case before."

Father Ibrahim chimed in, "But great Asshur, how many must be sacrificed?"

"This will not be a genocide. There are Assyrians in Iraq which will not be assets to the new Assyria... See this as a culling of the herd. You need to be patient and wait for my direction." replied Asshur.

Pul knelt and said, "As you command."

Asshur explained, "ISIS is a mix of men from many nations joined together in an attempt to kill or remove any non-Muslim people who wish to live within the Levant (Middle East). They as a group and as individuals are out of any direct control from any authority other than their own radical views. Islam is a jihad religion a war based belief. When these men are wound up and then released, it is nearly impossible to stop them. Even other Muslims will be their victims if they try to intercede. It will be necessary to defeat them militarily. This will be done by an international alliance and will take years to accomplish."

Pul grudgingly acknowledged what he had been told. his patience was wearing thin. But he had no choice.

In 2018, The Assyrian union was following developments in Mosul by the international military coalition. Finally, word came from the Iraqi government that ISIS had been completely driven out of Mosul, both the western and eastern parts were free. The battle left the city in ruins, entire sections were razed to the ground and nearly all the Christians had to flee.

Pul and Father Ibrahim are in Ermia, they met with some of Pul's spirit advisers in Pul's spirit office.

"The efforts of the international community have dissolved after ISIS was driven from Mosul and now, they turn their attention back to the civil war in Syria." Pul said.

Father Ibrahim replied, "The Iranians are building a presence in western Syria and is arming her surrogates in Lebanon. Iran wants to destroy Israel because they are a thorn in their side. Israel stands between them and their goal to establish a Shiite caliphate to control all the Middle East."

One of Pul's spirit counselors asked to speak. He was acknowledged, "Russia knows that Israel could defeat the Syrians and the Shiites if need be. So, they've placed Russian troops and equipment in and around Iranian and Syrian government troops to cause Israel to pause before acting. Any mistakes or miscalculations of any nation could set off a massive battle."

Another advisor asked to speak. Pul nodded. "This very situation has been anticipated by Israel for some time now. Their response was to acquire nukes. They have struggled with how to use them. Their first plan was to destroy themselves if their demise seemed imminent. This was called the Massada scenario. But now it seems that they have adopted a different plan, the Sampson scenario, they would use the nukes to destroy everyone around them. In effect, pulling down the columns of the Philistines, just like Sampson." [13]

The first adviser followed them up. "We don't know how they plan to deliver the nukes, we hear that they may plant them in strategic locations."

Even while this meeting was going on, a spirit messenger arrived at Pul's office and requested for an entry. After a few moments, he was brought in.

"Lord Assad... King of Syria has lost his temper with Israel because of their pressure against him and Hezbollah. He has launched a massive attack with his Russian built missiles, deep into Israel. Hezbollah and Hamas have followed suit." The spirit messenger said.

"What about Israel?" asked Pul.

The messenger added, "The first wave of the larger Syrian missiles were intercepted by the Israelis, some smaller missiles got thru but with little real effect. However, the second and third waves of Assad's missiles did get through along the coast from Gaza, up through Ashkelon and north to Tel Aviv. These did substantial damage."

"Have they surrendered?" Father Ibrahim asked.

The spirit looked down and then back up. "No"

"So, what are they doing?" the priest asked again.

"They've destroyed Damascus... nukes straight to the city center and out from there! Damascus is nothing but rubble, not even a city... Amman... and Tehran have been destroyed as well. [14][15][16]

There's an eerie silence over the Middle East... even the air waves were silent...

None of the other nations are saying anything. I think they're afraid to... they think they may be on Israel's kill list." The spirit stated.

The spirit adviser from Pul's meeting muttered, "Sampson"

After a few moments to collect their thoughts, Pul turned to Father Ibrahim and said, "Militant Islam has pushed too far. None of the remaining nations will be posturing. No high alerts. No threats, nothing. They won't provoke the Jews."

The messenger finished his report. "The armies in the field... Assad's, the rebels, Iranians, and Hezbollah have all stood down and began to move towards home." The spirit began to perk up a little when he says, Israel has not been untouched. Large areas along the coast were hit. It's obvious that the Jews pulled the trigger just in time. Any longer and there would not be an Israel." [17]

The news that Tehran was destroyed was disturbing to Pul and the rest of the union members. The union offices and files were in Tehran. However, just a week before, Asshur had warned Father Ibrahim, that he and Pul needed to remove as much of the critical information and people out of Tehran as they could.

"Go to Ermia," Asshur said.

This warning was not because of an Israeli attack, but because of an imminent asteroid and a second impact from a comet, coming from space to the earth. Pul and Father Ibrahim were somewhat baffled as to why Asshur had not seen the Israeli attack more clearly. They were however, gratified that the loss of life and damage was mitigated by the move.

The asteroid struck at a location in the south Atlantic and the Atlantic Ocean was devastated. Over sixty percent of the sea life was killed. The shipping was a total loss. The pollution was moving with the currents and the carnage was expanding.

The disturbance in the spirit realm was massive and Pul's meeting was quickly ended. Pul resorted to radio news for the time being.

Turkish radio announced, "As the world reels from the impact of the asteroid, a second alert was issued. This time it is a comet. It has hit between the border of India and Bangladesh. India, Pakistan and to the eastern coast of Africa. Over one billion dead. In just two weeks the entire world has been turned upside down." [18]

CHAPTER FIVE

Thomas Taylor

It was seven in the morning, of August 8, 1952, when Doctor Stevenson entered the recovery room at Mercy hospital in Oklahoma City. The night before, he had delivered a baby for a thirty-two year old woman, named Barbara Taylor. She had been brought in by an ambulance. He was there this morning to check her condition and to give her the good news. After assessing her physical condition and finding her stronger than he had expected. He decided to give her the good news.

"I thought I was going to lose you last night. But, I was able to save you and the baby, both. It doesn't always happen that way."

Barbara turned to the doctor and asked, "Is it a boy?"

The doctor replied, "Yes"

Barbara asked again, "Are you sure it's a boy?"

The nurse in the room explained to the doctor that Barbara had only recently woken up and could be slightly sedated.

"Yes, of course, why is it important?" the doctor replied.

"Only to me." Barbara explained and she continued, "I have three children, all girls. Now, I love my daughters very much but I would like to have a boy…for my husband's sake."

"Oh, he wants a boy?" Doctor Stevenson asked.

Barbara responded, "It's not quite that simple. Tom, my husband was killed two weeks ago in an oil field accident. He worked the rig."

"I'm sorry I didn't know." replied the doctor.

Barbara added, "I want my husband to have an heir, I want his name to continue. He was a good man and he loved God."

Five years later, in the tiny community of Okusa, Oklahoma, the community church, the only church within the town proper, was having their Sunday service.

The children and some of the youth groups went to a home, five houses down the street from the church to have their Sunday classes. The house was bought by the little church to help with overflow. This day was a beautiful late spring day and the children were playing games on the front lawn of the house. The favorite game was, "London Bridge Is Falling Down." When the games were finished, the teacher sat all the children down in front of him and gave them a short Bible lesson and it was straight-forward and to the point. The instructor explained how Jesus was taken to Calvary and crucified on the cross. He was crucified not because he was a bad man but rather because he needed to do it for the people who had done bad things. The teacher emphasized that Jesus died willingly. That he chose to die for everyone because he loved the people and wanted them to go to heaven when they die. He was then resurrected to prove that he was the Son of God.

Then the teacher asked the children, "Jesus died for you, will you live for Jesus?"

One of the children was a little five year old boy named, Thomas Taylor, the son of Barbara Taylor. Thomas was named after his father, who he never knew. Little Thomas's hand shot in the air.

"I'll live for Jesus." Thomas blurted out.

This surprised the teacher and he responded, "Tommy, you don't have to tell me. Just tell Jesus what you want and it's yours. It's all between you and Jesus."

Tommy may have been willing as a five year old boy to live for Jesus. As it was, he grew into a pretty typical teenager that certainly did not live for Jesus. He and his Okie friends spent most of their time down by the river fishing and drinking beer. Tommy never ran afoul of the law but several of his friends had. Tommy was adequate in school but never really applied himself. His mother, finally persuaded him to put in some effort and bring his grades up during his senior year of high school. He was able to get into a small community college near Oklahoma City. He fell in love with mathematics and engineering and for him it was a gift. He could see mathematical relationships and effects. For a young man in Oklahoma, the obvious industry for him was oil and gas as it paid well. He enjoyed the work and it would allow him to stay in the Oklahoma area.

One night, while he was with his college friends at a local watering hole in Oklahoma City, someone had brought up the subject of the value of going to church. Tom (he's not Tommy any more) was pretty much a conservative freedom kind of guy. Nothing was more important than a man's right to think and act independently. Big government was the biggest offender according to most of Tom's associates. But Tom found himself talking about organized religions. While governments controlled the society, economics and actions, religions restrict or control all the same things as government, except religions go deeper. Religion goes into how people think and their intentions. Religion demands that people conform to their set of beliefs or else. Tom's friends just stared at him, they had never seen him so forceful. His comments pretty much brought an end to the discussions.

Tom had been driving from school in Oklahoma City back home to Okusa every week-end. He would check in on his mom and took care of any jobs that needed doing around the house. It wasn't an extreme drive but it certainly gave him time to think. This evening was the second trip home since his comments with his friends. Tom had been perplexed by a certain uneasiness in his mind. Every time he thought about what he had said that night in Oklahoma City, he got a feeling that he had offended someone, *but who*? None of his friends had said anything, they seemed okay with everything. Tom drove along the two lane highway. There was almost no one else on the road, *who else goes to Okusa on a Friday night*? Then it happened, Tom's uneasiness blurted out.

"Leave me alone! Leave me alone!" The conflict within Tom's mind had erupted into open shouting, in the car. He continued, "God, if you're real then tell me... If you can't talk to me then you're not God. I'm not God yet I can talk! If you can show me that you're real... I will serve you all my life... In the meantime, leave me alone!" Tom exclaimed frustratingly.

This was no casual conversation. Tom was crying uncontrollably with tears flowing down his face. He had to pull over to the side of the road to recover his composure before going home. Tom decided not to tell anyone about the incident. He felt sure that they would not understand. He's not even sure that he wasn't cracking up. He told no one.

Back at school several weeks later, with the episode in the car behind him, Tom goes on with life as usual. Until one of his classmates asked him to go to a movie with him. It was his friends' birthday and his friend wanted to get away from studies. They went in and endured a perfectly boring film. But, as they were leaving the theater, they were moving slowly up the exit isle. Tom looked up and saw a spiritual vision right before him. The theater had opened up like a portal overhead. He saw two men sitting on thrones in a throne room.

The vision was gone as quickly as it came. But he saw them clearly and he knew who they were. The person in the center was a little higher than the one who was on his right. The one in the center was God himself, the Father. The person on the Father's right was Jesus, the son. Tom halted in his tracks momentarily, shocked. He then started moving with the crowd around him. He looked at the others who were literally all around him at the time to see if they had seen what he had seen. But, they just kept moving forward up the isle like cattle. He continued to keep glancing up at the ceiling as he walked out of the theater hoping for a second glimpse of the vision, but it was gone.

You might think that Tom would feel excited and elated to know that God is real. But Tom did not know where he stood. He was afraid that his past actions and words might exclude him from a relationship with God. Tom felt like God had every right to judge him and his sins, after all he had been indifferent to God's ways and laws. He had ignored God for years, and had even spoken against him. But one thing was clear, Tom had promised to serve God his whole life if God would reveal himself. And God certainly had done that.

Growing up in the Bible belt, Tom knew where to go to learn about God and Jesus, the Bible. Living in Okusa, he had been around the Bible all his life, but never bothered to see what it actually taught. He would dismiss what he heard as simple stories to keep the kids in line. Now, he was obligated to seriously search things out for himself. He needed to know what God expected.

Tom went back to the dorm that night and tried to sleep but he could not. His mind was racing, after all his entire world had just been turned upside down, his value system had taken a shot through the heart. Nothing seemed as valuable now as it was before, and spiritual things were suddenly a reality. He reasoned, that if Jesus is real then so is Satan, and hell. Tom was terrified at the thought of being held accountable for his sins. For the first time, he felt the spirit realm just outside his senses. Finally, from pure exhaustion he fell asleep, and slept right through his first two classes the next day. When he woke up, he decided to skip his other classes and drove home for the weekend. He knew he could not concentrate on something as mundane as calculus.

Tom was putting his bag in the back of his car, when some students walked by on the sidewalk in front of his car. They were laughing and talking, and then one of the students let out with a string of profanity and the others just laughed and continued walking. The words struck Tom like a slap in the face. He literally jerked around to see who said it. He wanted to shout, *Don't say that! Don't say those things!* But they were already too far down the walk. He said to himself, *"They don't know what I know. They don't know that God's real. They don't realize that God heard them blaspheme his name!"*

Then he heard a voice called his name, "Thomas, pray for them."

Tom was shocked to his very core, shivers were going up his back. *Who was that?* He thought. It was like the sound of a thought except, it wasn't his thought. This thought had come from someone else, from somewhere else, *but Who?* Tom looked around and saw no one else. Then he realized that only God would ask him to pray for those men! The voice was full of compassion not anger and whoever it was knew his name. Tears burst from Tom's eyes uncontrollably as he leaned over into the trunk of his car. He had just heard the voice of God! Tom nearly fell down when his knees went weak and he became dizzy, like a man with vertigo. He slowly regained himself and began to pray for the offending students. His prayer was simple and direct. He thought that if God can show compassion, he should too. He asked God to open their eyes that they might see. Then he gathered himself and began to drive himself back home. As Tom drove down the familiar two lane highway he heard the same voice again.

"Thomas pull over."

He looked for a place off the edge of the road, stopped and asked, "Yes, Lord."

"Thomas I have been talking to you for years. Every day, I have called to you. The problem was not whether I can talk but whether you can hear. You have been my son since that day on the church lawn, when you said you would live for me. Not one day have you been alone. You have ignored me but I have been with you."

Peace flowed through Tom like a river and all his fears melted away. From this time on, Tom was a changed man. He saw everything differently now. It was as if he had never really seen anything before. He saw and felt differently about people. He could see the superficial way people acted and their fears. He spoke to them with compassion and helped them see. He would study the Bible every moment he could. He began to learn all the doctrinal truths that he had spurned in his youth.

Tom finished his engineering degree because the Lord told him it was necessary. He decided to go to Bible College and learn the deeper things about God. Which he did, But he had difficulties because the Bible college was designed to train pastors and he did not feel that God wanted him to be a pastor. But, he still learned how to properly study scripture systematically. God showed him that his gift was in the area of prayer and intercession. He also had a keen interest in end time prophecies, those which speak of future events, things that are yet to happen.

Tom had worked for years in the engineering business and was well respected by his peers. His work was accurate and complete. At one point he had just finished a large multi-year project, and his employer was waiting for another large project to start. His company had decided to furlough Tom and some others in his work group. He was placed on paid leave for five full months. Tom was able to immerse himself all day to studying prophecy. He studied all the prophets and their books, every word, every reference. He researched word meanings and charted all his findings. With the Lord's help, he was seeing things that he had completely missed before, making connections that clarified many of his questions. His personal understanding of the prophecies and their implications became clearer than ever before. These five months turned out to be an opportunity of a lifetime.

Tom soon found out that just because something he has studied seemed clear to him, it doesn't mean others will also see it the way he did. Some teachers and professors were not quick to affirm his findings. They weren't harsh or unkind to him. But they told him to keep his findings to himself for a while and they would have to wait and see how things will develop. Tom remembered what his teacher on the church lawn told him years ago. *"Tommy don't tell me. Tell Jesus. It's between you and Jesus."* But Tom isn't five years old anymore. He wrote it all down in books and charts and in every way he could and taught anyone who would listen.

Tom lived and worked in Oklahoma City until 2014. His mother had died in 2004 and his youngest sister Mary was taking care of the family home in Okusa. Tom, now 62 years old and prepared to retire. He wanted to go home and so he made arrangements with Mary to take the house and live there on his own. He spent the last year renovating the house. He made himself a study and library that anyone would be proud of.

He had a retirement party at his office. The company was particularly generous to him when he left, but of all the gifts he received, the one he liked the most was a specialty pen which was carved from exotic wood and had his name engraved in the shaft. The pen came with additional ink replacement cartridges. It was simply a beautiful pen and it made a thick jet black line. He used the pen to write nearly all his works, papers and manuscripts.

When Tom returned to Okusa he found that the community church had a new pastor named, John. Tom went over to the church to meet him. He was very pleased when he talked to him. This young man had a deep and sincere love for God. He also had a love for God's word, specifically, prophecy. The more Tom talked to Pastor John the more he understood that this young man had a deep understanding of the things of God. The two became prayer and study partners. Pastor John was a great communicator and soon had the little community buzzing at the eminence of the Lord's return to collect the dead in Christ, and those who are alive and remaining on earth. John was willing to put his reputation on the line for his convictions. There was a true revival taking place in Okusa. The Holy Spirit honored the prayers and did great things in this little community and church. Entire families were being touched and brought to the Lord.

One of the areas of prophecy that Tom had been following closely was the coming of an Assyrian man who would become a world leader. He would be a man of peace early in his career and then later become a dictator. With the advent of the internet, Thomas was able to look for a man that might fit the Biblical description. Thomas began to follow things about the coming new Assyria and the man that will lead it.

One afternoon, Tom just finished praying and was preparing to study, when a news flash came on the TV news channel. It said that Damascus had just been destroyed by an attack from Israel. The details were sketchy but the attack had indeed happened. Tom stood to his feet and moved to his computers. He turned them on and started searching for more news. He knew what this attack meant. It meant that the Lord's return would happen very soon. He used his favorite pen and began writing notes as the information became available. He took a chart that showed the next event to be the resurrection of the dead and living believers. He took his pen and drew an "X" on the diagram and wrote, *"We are here."* Thomas set his pen down, bowed his head and began to pray.

CHAPTER SIX

Nineveh Assyria's New Capital

Just days after the destruction of Damascus, Pul received a summons from Asshur, that he was to appear before him at the top node of the tree of life. Pul complied.

Asshur began, "Sharrukinbanipal, the time is now, right. Go to Baghdad and talk to the prime minister of Iraq. He will be expecting you. You are to demand that the Assyrians receive their homeland and full autonomy. You will require all of Bet Nahrain (the land of Nineveh) and all the land west to Ermia. This will include Mosul and Arbel. The old city of Nineveh will be your new capital. Go into the old walls and rebuild it."

"Might the Iraqi government find this too bold, Father?" asked Pul.

Asshur shouted at Pul. "No! They fear a civil war like Syria's. Never question me again! Do it now!"

"As you command." Pul muttered.

Three months later, in an Assyrian Union meeting in a hotel in Mosul, only a small distance from the old city walls of Nineveh. Pul was at the epicenter of the lively celebration. Pul raised a glass of Arak in front of a room full of Assyrian zealots. [19][20]

Pul toasted, "Gentlemen, I have fought and clawed and sacrificed for all of Assyria, and now it has all lead up to this. We will move into our new nation in Iraq and begin to set up government in Nineveh!"

Cheers all around.

Almost immediately, money and resources began to flow into Pul and his new government. Some of it was from Assyrians around the world supporting the new Assyria. But, most of it was coming from spiritual blackmail by Asshur and his minions. They were pressuring individuals, corporations and even governments all over the world which had received assets or favors from Asshur over the years. It seemed the day of reckoning has come.

Money was initially spent on securing the oil fields within the land. Oil alone could fund a new start-up government. But Pul was also flowing money back to the people themselves. Not only building funds and no taxes, but also as direct personal wealth. This policy was unheard of in the Middle East. Pul was even asked by the Iranians to lead Iran after their destruction. The old Islamic Republic had been an utter failure economically. The people desperately needed relief. Pul was instantly, wildly popular in Iraq and Iran.

Pul, the little Assyrian boy from Ermia has become the leader of Assyria, Northern Iraq, and Iran. The celebration continued. Pul's associates all joined in singing the Assyrian national anthem. Pul and Father Ibrahim stepped away and started a private conversation.

Pul began, "Father, I expected that there would be a certain level of satisfaction in my accomplishments, but... I've come to realize that Asshur wants more from me. More than just an Assyrian national leader."

Father Ibrahim initially looked pleased and asked, "Perhaps an Assyrian empire?"

Pul replied with false surprise, "Now that's a very interesting idea." It's clear that Pul had given it a lot of thought.

Father Ibrahim showed a look of concern. "Would this empire have a place for me?"

"Yes! Of course, right with me, up front and center. In fact, you must promise to stay and counsel me all the way." Pul continued, "This is all very good news to me. I still feel strong and healthy. Father, I want greater things. My powers and ambitions are stronger than ever before. I feel unstoppable." Pul marveled.

Four months later. Pul was working hard. He shared time between his Mosul Nineveh office and his prime minister's office in Iran. But his pleasure was in Nineveh. The old city of Nineveh was literally inside of the eastern portion of the modern city of Mosul. While the city of Mosul was nearly razed to the ground by ISIS. It is now being rebuilt by a massive international effort. Pul was concentrating on Nineveh. He wanted to make it his Assyrian government citadel. The ruins that were called Nineveh were only being used for agricultural purposes. Pul received some push back from the archeological world for building on top of the old city, but Pul could not be swayed. In a speech Pul made a case.

"Israel uses the old city of Jerusalem, Rome is still used by the Italians, and the old walled city of York is still used by the English. Why can't the Assyrians rebuild Nineveh? We as Assyrians are not looking to the past for our focus, but to the future. We will of course respect what we find and preserve it, but not in the British museum or Chicago! Now it will stay home." By the time Pul was through with his speech, he wagged his finger at the camera.

The old Nineveh was nearly two miles square. And was still enclosed by walls and gates. The old gates were gone but Pul rebuilt the gate structure and hung new modern security gates. The old walls were not all vertical. Some areas were reduced to rounded mud ramparts, but Pul was reinforcing all the existing stone and brick structures and then added modern steel fencing and shields on top. This included new military guard structures and walkways for troop movements. He was also placing steel buildings inside the city to house the new government and garrison the fledgling Assyrian military. These buildings are to be temporary and will be upgraded as soon as time allows. A water plant and power plant were quickly brought on line. He also rebuilt the ancient tower located at the city center.

CHAPTER SEVEN

NATO The Spear Head

In the television news studio of a BBC news show, that was similar to Larry King live. The British interviewer begins, "Welcome back, before the advertisement break, we were talking with General Clarke of NATO, the North Atlantic Treaty Organization. So back to our topic. I have an excerpt here from the Jerusalem post, which says NATO has moved a special military force into the Middle East in an attempt to stabilize the region from descending into a war lord feudal system. This force is called the Rapid Deployment Force, correct?"

General Clarke replied, "Yes, it is very robust and dynamic. It consists of—"

The interviewer interrupted, "Many refer to them as the head of the spear."[21][22]

The General glossed over the comment and added, "It consists of forces from ten NATO member and partner nations. Five from Europe and five from the Middle East, including Turkey. They consist of ten commanders or Generals which understand situational tactics and know how to respond to dynamic circumstances. These commanders operate with near autonomy when in the combat theater."

"It seems to me like the five commanders from the Muslim nations are an attempt to make sure that the Muslims don't feel like this is an occupying force from Europe, you know crusaders." The interviewer remarked.

"I have to admit that the force is being resisted by many in the region because they are not comfortable with a purely military force without any direct, real time, civilian oversight. We are currently looking for someone that is acceptable to everyone involved, this will not be easy." The general added.

Just days later, Pul outside his Nineveh office was being interviewed by a TV news crew.

"The question has been asked, who would be acceptable to both Jews and Muslims?" the reporter stated.

Pul responds "I understand the Muslim concerns because of my position in the Iranian Government, but I'm not a Muslim, but rather a Christian. And more than that. An Assyrian, a Semite." [23]

"It seems you are someone that both Jews and Muslims respect, as well as a man highly regarded in Iran and now in Iraq. It's easy to see how your name was brought forth." said the reporter.

"Oh, you're too kind..." This comment gets a legitimate laugh from the others in the room.

Pul continued, "So, as I was saying, NATO has approached me and it was really an easy answer... I accepted the position. This is what my father would have wanted." Pul sent a knowing glance at Father Ibrahim, who was standing against the back wall.

"Thank you again for your time, sir. I wish you all the best and good luck with your new position in NATO!" remarked the reporter.

Pul turned to the cameras with a wide shark like grin. The cameras flashed.

NATO headquarters in Brussels Belgium. Pul was conducting a briefing for the international news media. This was after his tasks and direction had been established by NATO. Pul was at a podium and again lights were flashing.

Pul stated, "The first task I will undertake is to get all the nations in the area which still have functioning governments to agree to allow my NATO forces to be the only military force operating in the area. All military or paramilitary units will have to stand down and disarm."[24]

The international and local journalists recorded, and took notes. It's a mixed bag of reactions.

Pul continued, "In exchange, NATO will provide security to all nations... I repeat all nations in the Levant without any actions to be taken based on race or religion. We will simply provide security for all concerned. This security agreement will be a temporary arrangement which will be reassessed at the end of seven years... We believe this is a sufficient time to start rebuilding and establishing home rule governments." He continued, "NATO forces would have the right to enter into, and inspect any nation... at any time... unannounced, and remain until any civil unrest is mitigated. They can also keep, if necessary, garrisons within any nation they choose."

The Media burst into questions, an overwhelming situation. Pul just smiled and put his hands in the air, turned and walked away. The technique he learned from the priests in Ermia. It worked in Brussels as well.

Pul spent the next two weeks reviewing his forces which were already deployed in the Levant (Middle East). He travelled with his ten commanders and their support staff. He entered and consulted with all the nations and their leadership. He was amazed at how robust his forces were. They were the best NATO had to offer. They intimidated everyone who saw them. Pul most liked it when they all saluted him.

Pul finished his tour and returned home to Nineveh. He was in a new office built by NATO within the Old Nineveh walls. It was separate but adjacent to his Assyrian government offices.

Pul didn't think much of it. He said it had no class and no taste. But Father Ibrahim reminded him that no one else in the world holds the position that he does and that offices come and go. The priest promised him that the next one will be better.

A NATO officer stood in front of Pul reading updates from the Levant.

NATO officer announced, "Kuwait, the UAE, Bahrain, Saudi Arabia, Qatar and even Oman have accepted the terms very quickly."

"But?" asked Pul.

The officer continued, "Iraq, Egypt and Israel did not just jump on board. These nations have a lot to lose by allowing their military to be dismantled or put into mothballs for seven years."

Pul looks at Father Ibrahim who sat at the back of the office, monitoring.

Father Ibrahim spoke to the officer. "Iraq will bend very soon to American pressure. Please add that to your report for tomorrow's meeting."

The officer flinched and frowned. This comment from a priest was a break in protocol, and he doesn't quite know how to take it. He looked at Pul for direction. Pul simply nodded his approval. It's clear that this priest does more than taking confessions. He looked like a priest but talked like a general.

"You can go." exclaimed the priest.

"Thank you for your efforts. Have a good evening." remarked Pul.

The officer saluted and left.

Father Ibrahim moved over to Pul's desk and sat directly across from him and with a very direct look, said, "Israel and Egypt will not be so easily shaken."

"Don't worry, I have a bargaining chip for Israel." Pul replied.

"You know what you must do."

"Yes, even if I have to call on all my powers... I will get the answers I want... I will not be deterred." Pul stated.

CHAPTER EIGHT

The Jewish Temple

Pul was in his Nineveh office. The TV was on, and a news reporter was on location at the temple mount in Jerusalem. A structure was being put in place behind her. [25]

A news reporter announced, "After over two thousand years the Jews will sacrifice again. Back in 1994, The Jews built a temple at a remote underground site in the Colorado Rocky Mountains. All the stone tool work and gold fabrication was done there. Then it was disassembled and shipped covertly to Israel. It was placed in hiding at an archaeological site near Jerusalem. The temple proper is not really that large. It's about forty-five feet wide and ninety feet long and three stories high." The reporter continued, "As you can see behind me, construction workers are placing the final stones in place and adding the interior panels and furniture. The Israelis have put the temple shell in place within forty eight hours of signing the NATO security agreement with NATO representative Pul Bet Sharrukin."

The TV cameras panned around to show the activity on the mount. The news reporter walked to a group of Jewish priests and rabbis. He interviewed the one in charge.

"So... What's the arrangement?" asked the reporter.

The Jewish priest answered, "Mr. Bet Sharrukin decided to offer Israel a location on the temple mount for a Jewish temple. The Muslim structures on the site will remain and the Jews will control the northern part of the site. A wall of separation would be built between us... We have reluctantly agreed. But to be perfectly honest, at first we abhorred this compromise... But we simply could not resist the possibility of a temple."[26]

The news reporter asked again, "But, what about the Muslims? How do they feel about it?"

The Jewish priest replied, "Since the last conflict, the Muslims have become more flexible and much more open to peace with Israel, including the new temple. So long as the existing Muslim mosques are not touched and they still have access to them, they are okay with the arrangement."

The camera panned back around to the reporter standing in front of the new temple.

"Jews all over the world are rejoicing. Symbolic or religious, this structure is uniting Jews all over the world." The news reporter stated.

The TV went black. Pul was in a simmering rage.

Later that night, we found Pul and Father Ibrahim in Pul's modern and expensive living room. The room was disheveled by a storm, Pul was the storm. Father Ibrahim tried his best not to be affected.

"Within a few weeks they'll dedicate the temple and start daily sacrifices." He told Pul.

"They had obviously been planning for this day. They had already trained the priests. They had the furniture and tools ready to go!" Pul yelled.

"You made a great mistake." Father Ibrahim spoke.

"It was not my intent to promote or bless Israel! I figured it would take years for the different Jewish sects to come to some sort of agreement on how to proceed, who knew?" Pul responded.

"I have hopes you'll do better with Egypt. Is the prime minister still resistant to signing the agreement?" asked Father Ibrahim.

"I even sat down face to face with him. We smiled and exchanged pleasantries, but I could not make any progress." Pul stated. He took a shot of Arak, (a strong alcoholic drink, which is clear until mixed with water) and continued, "Then finally, my spirit helpers informed me that he was lying to me on many accounts. There was no chance of him relenting."[27]

"Without Egypt's participation in the NATO project, the entire endeavor will fall apart. They must be made to yield!" the priest belted.

Pul threw his glass across the room. He screamed in the spirit. "How dare this man refuse to submit to me. He does not understand who I am... I am the Son of Asshur!"

CHAPTER NINE

The Missing People

In Oklahoma, USA. A news van drove past an arched metal sign post, *"Welcome to Okusa."* About fifty yards further along there was another small sign saying, *"Jesus Saves - Okusa Community Church."*

The van had three people inside, all in their 20's. On the wheel, Evelyn Odel, a communications expert. Evelyn looked like the girl next door, 5'6" with short brown hair and dark brown eyes. She has a Mediterranean complexion.

In the back of the van, with the equipment was a British video camera operator, Isaac Warren. He's a 23 year old Englishman, black hair combed straight back, with hazel eyes. He's tall and lanky, but still athletic. He was a British national but left his family in Britain to work at Washington, D.C.

Riding shotgun was reporter/journalist, Laura Thornton. She was definitely camera ready. A slim 5'8" with blond mid-length hair and fair complexion. Laura was scrolling down Google Images viewing well-maintained buildings, Indian-themed souvenirs in tourist heavy shops, smiling locals in quaint cafes, open grass lands. An idyllic Midwestern town.

A call popped up from Sean Wright, the Producer. He asked, "Where are you guys?"

"What?" Laura tapped Evelyn on the shoulder. "We're on Cran Street."

Sean gave Evelyn his position.

"Got it we'll be there in 15..." Evelyn responded.

Isaac Warren looked out the window and blurted out. "Whoa..."

Laura distracted by Isaac. "Hold tight we'll be there soon... bye." Laura told Sean.

They slowed and looked. Cars were parked outside pristine commercial buildings, but no one on the sidewalks. No one in the shops. No one in the park. A true ghost town. Deserted. Abandoned.

Evelyn whispered, "Unreal... so eerie."

Then Isaac blurted out, "Stop, stop! We need to get a shot of this."

The van was parked but still running. The door slid shut revealing CHANNEL.7.D.C. I-TEAM written on the side.

Evelyn was still in the driver's seat, looking out. Isaac pointed a bulky camera at Laura who's getting ready in front of a deserted street.

"3, 2, 1 and..." Isaac counted down.

Laura began, "During the aftermath of two major astrological disasters, and war in the Middle East, over a billion people have been killed. But it comes to light that some, perhaps tens of thousands, have simply disappeared all over the world. Many think that most of them have gone into hiding–believing that the only safe place would be in shelters or underground. The Channel 7 News Investigative Team have come to Okusa, Oklahoma where everyone has virtually disappeared."

Isaac said, "Cut." But as he did, a cutting wind blew. His arm hairs stood on end. He added, "OK that's it, I'm out of here... let's go. We got what we need."

Laura laughed, "Oh no you don't... The 'I' in I team means Investigate. Come on! We've got a job to do."

The van arrived at an intersection, coming up finally to three people on lounge chairs sitting on someone's lawn.

They met the rest of the team. Producer Sean Wright, 28, short blond hair and with intense blue eyes. He has a stout build and there's no doubt he's in charge although perpetually stressed.

Sally Hamilton, the still camera photographer. She could be Laura's younger sister, she's a little shorter and has lighter hair, that she kept short for convenience.

And Gus G. Hubbard, the investigator. He's 42, a no nonsense man with dark brown eyes and brown hair, a big man, 6'2, 200 lbs. with a perpetual five o' clock shadow. He's honest to a fault. He's just finalized his divorce and not at all happy. He's with the team to help them read clues.

They re-united as a team. Handshakes and polite smiles, still professional.

Laura asked Sean, "Tell me you found those shelters..."

"I'm sorry to disappoint you." Sean answered.

"Come on at least someone? Anything?" asked Evelyn.

Sean explained, "No one at all. Not even the handful of residents which first reported the disappearance. They've left and refused to return at all."[28] Sean turned to Gus. "You go with Isaac. Sally goes with Evelyn. Laura, you come with me. Its better you guys see for yourselves."

The team began to explore the neighborhood. Gus led Isaac to the pathway of the house behind them. Truck still parked on the driveway. Isaac peeked through the window. The TV was on the news channel.

In another home. Evelyn opened a fridge. It's well-stocked. The produce box had fruits and veggies inside. Sally took a picture.

Sean opened a closet, bathroom and bedroom. He sees the clothes were folded, toiletries were there and a bed that was made.

Later in the day, they were on Cran Street as they approached the fourth house.

The street lights turned on. They stopped in their tracks.

"All right, let's make this the last stop. We'll spend the night here. Take your pick." Sean spoke. He looked around the other homes. Lights still on. Seemingly just another day winding down.

Laura points, "That one's as good as any, I guess."

Sean, "Laura, call Eve to get the van 'round."

The crew entered with their back packs and bags. A decent middle class home but somehow different. There is a family photo on the piano. They made themselves feel at home. Some were exploring. Some on the couch, tired but minds racing.

Gus was perplexed. "If we're just basing this on the evidence, these people fled from their homes quickly, on foot or at least we're given rides to their destination by someone else. Their own vehicles are still here."

"The thing is, I didn't see signs of a rush. No one even bothered to take their belongings or valuables." added Laura.

"If you were going to hide, you wouldn't leave your food behind... or your clothes, right? But they did. They even left their guns." Gus continued.

Isaac appeared from the hallway, wide-eyed. "You won't believe this. You won't believe this..." Isaac led the others into the owner's study. Books everywhere, charts and pictures on the walls. The computers on the desk were still on, and an open Bible.

Gus remarked, "This is just another one those Bible people."

Evelyn was at the desk going through the owner's PC's. "Those aren't even half of it, Laura come here."

Laura responded, "No! That's just a major breech of privacy."

"What? These computers were all on when we got here. Just look at this Laura. There are dozens of pictures and news articles. The owner here has been following the career of some Assyrian big shot." Evelyn explained.

"You mean a Syrian right?" asked Laura.

Evelyn answered, "No, evidently there's a difference, and Assyrians still exist in Iran and Iraq. There're tons of this stuff! Look, detailed charts are all over, scroll there, there... These are all recent events in the Middle East... Wait, are those Biblical verses?" She continued, "Yup. All from the Jewish prophets which 'foretold' all those events."

Sean came up behind them. holding a pen that he found on the desk. He instinctively slipped it into his shirt pocket and said, "We also found files where he showed the events that are still to come, even the order he believed they would happen."

Laura responded, "So, Sean you're saying these charts are supposed to be a guide to the future events of the world?"

Isaac and Sally found a time line of events laying on the desk, an X mark with a dark pen. "We are here." The X indicated, "The removal of the Bride of Christ."

Sally read, "They which are alive and remain shall be caught up to the clouds in a moment in the twinkling of an eye. We shall all be changed. Only those who were looking for Christ's return would hear his voice and that no one else would see the event. It will be a mystery."[29]

Isaac began to mock the old man. "Oh boy!"

Gus joined in. "You can keep your Bible and all its fairy tales."

Evelyn rolled her eyes at the two guys and handed Isaac a thick external hard drive.

Isaac asked, "What is this?"

"It's three terabytes of backed up data, charts, commentaries and photos. The whole shebang." Evelyn answered.

"Hey! We can't just be taking this guy's stuff!" Isaac exclaimed.

Evelyn turned to Sally. "Back me up on this."

"I say take it." Sally stated.

Gus went through one of the books on the shelf. *"D.C."* on the spine. In the front page was, *"Property of Thomas Taylor"*. "Whoa! Look what I've got here..." exclaimed Gus.

They all gathered behind him. Peering over Gus with the large book. He started flipping pages. A very detailed map of Washington with indications of cryptic symbols and hand written details.

Laura turned to Sean and said, "We've got to verify this!"

"Don't tell me you guys are really considering this?" asked Gus.

Laura, turns to Gus "We are collecting evidence and data, If you find some other explanation for this, let me know. We'll take it too. But for right now this is all we've got."

Sean gathered the whole team in the living room. "We need to get a consensus on what we are going to report back to the agency. Here is how I see it. The people appear to have left their homes willingly and left with others of their community. They left to a place of refuge which we could not locate, but it appears to be a remote location which is some distance away. There is also no indication of when or if they will return, and no indication of foul play of any kind." Sean stared at the others then he continued, "I think that anything beyond these facts would be speculation on our part. I also feel we should not tell anyone about the idea that God may have removed them. That could ruin our careers. Also, don't show anyone else the data we've collected." To Sean's surprise he got his consensus from the others.

Later that week, the crew returned to their news agency in D.C. The station's head producer, Karen Newton, went through the crew's report and research. She shot Sean a suspicious gaze. "You've got to be kidding me?"

Sean explains "These people left their homes willingly to a place of refuge. It's all right there."

"So, you're sure... They're not dead?" Karen suspiciously asked.

"There's no evidence that they're dead... I don't think so." Sean kept his cool.

Sean went home to his apartment where the others in the team were conducting research. When he arrived, he hardly got a reaction from Evelyn and Gus. They were glued to their Laptops.

"Did you two even sleep?" asked Sean.

"Well... I hate to say it... The symbols are everywhere." Gus stated.

Evelyn faced her monitor to Sean. A shaky phone camera video of Laura inside the statuary hall at the Capitol building. It panned to a statue of a woman with an eagle attending beside her. [30] It zoomed in at the left of the statue.

"A broken column with a serpent coiled around it." The camera pointed back to Laura who had her phone up. It was a photo taken from the book. "A snake coiled." Laura added.

Isaac spoke, "Would you look at that..." The video stopped and rewound to the frame with the snake on the column.

"According to Thomas' book, the interpretation of the medallion is, 'Nimrod's Babylon will die and will appear dead but will be revived by Lucifer at some point in the future.'" Evelyn reported.

Gus explains "The snake is named Helios... Lucifer in Hebrew. He emphasizes that Helios around the broken column represents a broken nation and the new nation is revealed at the center." Gus rewound back to the statue of the woman and eagle, and said, "America is the daughter of Babylon."

"Aren't you just stretching this?" asked Sean.

"No, I believe this is intentional. The symbols are too precise to be just chance. I don't know what it actually means, but I know what they intended for them to mean." Gus replied.

Evelyn started a slide show of statues.

Gus added, "These are from Sally. Taken from the government buildings around Washington D.C. Statues of the woman America and the eagle with a nude youth, and Genius, a presiding spirit. There are Pagan god's everywhere, just look at it." [31]

The slides continued. A photo of a painting at the center of the Capitol Rotunda with George Washington at the center of a heavenly scene. Circled around him are Roman/Greek gods and goddesses instructing the American forefathers. [32]

"No reference of the Biblical God. Everything was just as the data Thomas Taylor indicated. And Sean..." Evelyn spoke as she opened the book to a bookmarked page. She handed it to Sean.

He sighs and said, "Gather everyone here tonight."

The crew were at Sean's apartment that night and huddled over dinner.

Isaac shrugs his shoulders "It's crazy... I've never even given those statues or paintings any thought. I've been stationed here for years!"

Laura remarked, "What's disturbing is that, I've been monitoring the news recently with the government research we're verifying. I have to admit, now I'm seeing the anti-God bias of the government like never before."

"The conclusion... This guy Thomas wrote that a secret organization was responsible for the founding of America... A secret esoteric religious group which is not orthodox Christian." Evelyn concludes.

"The laws of America were Judeo-Christian because most of the population were Christian... And would not accept anything else." Laura added.

Sally chimed in, "If you think about it, the American government was designed to allow the laws to change as the people wished. The government could-over time-take God out of the laws and replace them with humanist thinking... or whatever."

"Right, it is this perversion of God's laws that the Bible indicated will be the reason why God will destroy America. God would remove his protection that has been over America... From her creation. And that even if America should place her national defenses in space the destruction would be successful." Evelyn said.

Sean was reading the book and jotting down notes, when he realized he's using the pen that he found in the study of Thomas Taylor, "Oh man, I took his pen... Oh well too late now." Sean continued reading the book. "The thing that shook me was that Thomas actually listed down the nations involved in the attack and destruction of America. An assembly of great nations, Russia, Iran, Ethiopia and the ten commander-Generals associated with the ten nations of NATO!"[33]

Gus interrupted, "Now, now... While this information is all very interesting, let's not go jumping into bunkers. It only proves that the Christian researcher from Oklahoma was thorough and persuasive in his studies. It does not mean that there is a God... Or that God is going to destroy anything."

"One thing that is happening..." Sally remarks, "I'm pretty sure we're all beginning to see things... The world differently."

"Eve, you said you have something to show us?..." asked Sean.

Eve turned on the projector on a bare wall. It had the charts which had been prepared with scriptures that applied and the order in which events would happen.

"Take note that the destruction of America won't happen next." Gus indictated.

Evelyn explains, "The nation of Egypt is to be the next major event. Egypt would be destroyed... Burned by fire... From the north to the south and uninhabited for 40 years."[34]

Isaac laughed, "Well, that settles it. Unless Egypt goes kaboom there's no reason for us to worry about America!"

CHAPTER TEN

Egypt, The Canal is Mine

Pul was at a meeting in Jerusalem with Israeli government representatives.

Their eyes converged on Pul, judging, simmering.

The Israeli leader stated, "Within a week of your meeting with Egypt, Egypt has issued a statement that they were acting on their sovereign rights to restrict Israel's use of the Suez Canal and to anyone else they chose to."[35]

Pul injects, "Egypt had made it clear that they weren't a part of the Levant. They are in Africa and are an independent nation. I pointed out that the Sinai Peninsula is in the Levant and Egypt claims it as theirs."

The Israeli representative exclaimed, "We have a peace agreement with Egypt that requires that Israel have open use of the canal for commercial and military use... Without exception!"

Pul was silently fighting the mounting pressure, then said, "Please understand, at first, I was simply irritated that they did it, and at this point I'm still not too upset. Egypt is simply pushing back at me."[36]

"It's not all about you, the Israeli representative exclaimed, the agreement is a peace treaty! Do you know what that means?! If Egypt breaks the treaty it would be an act of war! We demand that you and NATO represent Israel to the Egyptians! Israel wants to know what good is our defense security agreement with NATO if the first time there is a problem, you do nothing!"

Pul composed himself coolly and took deep breaths. "It's clear that I'm being pushed to act. After clarifying Egypt's position and being sure that they are entrenched in it, my ten generals and I will begin planning a response to restore Israel's use of the canal. Israel has already destroyed several nations because of Israel's imminent destruction. Egypt is not looking for more war."

The Israeli's mood changed. He stood down.

Pul cannot move against Egypt without approval from Asshur. Pul was in Asshur's throne room, in front of his altar. "Father, I ask for your spiritual approval to move against Egypt..."

"My son... This battle needs to be done... This is my order to you. Move quickly and also have a plan made with NATO Europe. Have them prepare to end the conflict if things go badly. Eliminate Egypt's military and government, you can use tactical nuclear weapons if needed. But do not consult Israel!" Asshur commanded.

"Thank you Father. Everyone in NATO agrees that if Egypt fights back there should be no Egypt left when it's all over. After all, they are the ones who closed the canal and broke the treaty." Pul bowed and backed away from the throne.

Two weeks later, Pul and the spearhead forces were prepared to move against the Egyptians, Pul's forces were in the Negev desert just inside the Israeli border.

Pul spoke into the field radio. "Commence the operation."

Pul's tanks and armored vehicles were the latest European and American weapons. Clearly, the advantage lies with NATO and Pul's troops.

The Egyptian forces moved to engage but soon realized it is futile. After, the front echelon of the Egyptians began to suffer loses. They moved back very quickly. Pul's blitz pushed them back to the Canal in just hours.

The general who was with Pul told him, "We've arrived sir. Do you want to proceed?"

"Yes, of course, seize the canal and then push on to Cairo." Pul ordered.

Pul crossed the canal on one of his many temporary bridges. Feeling victorious, he wanted to teach the Egyptians a lesson. He did not realize that the Egyptians have hidden troops and equipment in emplacements spreading along the west bank of the canal. The Egyptians allowed Pul and most of his forces to pass right by without a fight or detection. Pul and his men travelled all the way to Cairo, the city was nearly deserted. Pul's men looted treasures and valuables piling into vehicles. Pul looked on, consenting. [37]

Then, Pul heard his spirit consorts whispered to him. "The Egyptians are about to spring an ambush that will destroy the NATO Forces!" Pul's eyes darted everywhere.

"What is it?! Where?!" Pul shouted.

Back at the canal border, the Egyptian troops were mustered. They closed in to block the path of retreat.

Pul's spirits urged him, "Withdraw immediately! There's no time to wait!"

The larger Egyptian army began to engage Pul's rear guard.

Pul dashed to a commander and shouted, "Go! Go! Go! It's a trap."

They raced the Egyptians to the choke points. Knowing they may not escape.

Pul got on the field radio, and gave the order to NATO. "Call down fire on Egypt!"

As Pul and his forces slipped back into the Negev. The rumbling and shaking can be heard. Smoke began to rise in the west. Cairo was destroyed. The Egyptian sea coast and the entire Nile valley was burned behind them. Then silence. No one cheered, faces were blank, and no one talked. It was as if the only noise was the mechanical clanking of tank tracks. Later that day, they stopped in the Negev near some sand dunes to reform the equipment and organize for the trip home. From the dunes came two armored cars and a military jeep. The Israelis came out to meet Pul. They were furious, they had not been consulted.

"We did not expect you and NATO to destroy Egypt! The canal was a diplomatic problem not an excuse for war!" yelled one of the Israelis.

Pul's eyes were locked with the Israeli. Pul's eyes, the eyes of a beast. He ordered his commander, "Lead the troops back to Assyria."

"Yes sir." They turned and left.

Later that night, they camped in northern Arabia. In Pul's command tent, he paced on the edge. His commanders fed off the rage. Pul did not feel anger against Asshur who told him to destroy Egypt. Instead, he blamed Israel who he hated.

"How dare they! I'm doing their dirty work! They told me to do something and I did!" Pul shouted.

One of his commanders approached him and exclaimed, "We concur with you on all points. Those Jews used you to save themselves at the expense of Egypt!"

Another commander stood up and spoke, "You would not have done it if it weren't for the security agreement."

Pul muttered, "All these covenant Jews and Christians. I would kill them all if I could."[38]

The commanders' approached Pul and said, "Give us the direct order, sir... We will turn back to Israel and destroy her!"

Pul stood to his feet and commanded, "Make the plans for the approach to Israel!"[39]

The generals all stood up and saluted Pul.

They cleared the tables, maps and charts laid out. Pul smirked, totally vindicated.

The next day, military vehicles began to move towards the west, to Israel. Pul in his command vehicle stared out the window when the commander with him handed him the field phone.

"From NATO HQ, sir. The Americans are demanding you stand down and withdraw!" said the commander.

"What right do the Americans have in meddling in my affairs?!" asked Pul.

"It seems that Israel still has an ally. You do understand that the Americans could make short work of us, should they want to?" the commander replies.

"They should keep their values to themselves." Muttered Pul.

"Sir! There are three American aircraft carriers setting off the coast of Israel! Awaiting orders, sir..." The commander informed. [40]

Pul muttered, "I will come back and when I do, no one will be able to stop me!"

Weeks later, at a meeting and dinner in Pul's personal residence in Nineveh. The dinner guests were ten hardened men of different nationalities. They're Pul's military strike group. [41]

Pul spoke, "I thank you all again for joining me, gentlemen." He raised his glass. "Now, allow me to get to business. I need to get input. What might be done to destroy Israel?" [42]

The four Arab partners were quick and said, "We've been trying to destroy her for years. Perhaps our northern commanders will do better than us."

"Yes, we must." agreed Pul.

The first northern commander responded, "For many years NATO has been an uncertain alliance. We may use this to our advantage."

"Go on..." Pul said.

The commander continued, "Alliances must have common goals in order to be strong when under pressure. Early in the alliance the enemy and the goals were clear, to keep the Soviet Union out of Western Europe. But since the fall of the Soviet Union in the 90's, America and European NATO have often disagreed. The United States had to operate unilaterally more and more as European NATO would drag their feet. For the Europeans needed, or at least wanted the American dollars. So, no official change in policy."

Pul asked, "So NATO has little or no clout to make America move one way or another?"

"Correct! The only advantage they have on the Americans is, the alliance itself. The Europeans are intimate with America's military and defenses. They have all the codes and strategies for defense. To put it plainly..." The commander explained.

Pul interrupted, "They could betray America... and she could be destroyed..."

A second northern commander entered the conversation. "But NATO Europe does not have the necessary number of assets (Nukes) required to guarantee a total victory. The United States is a massive nation with industry and population centers all over. So, NATO would eventually need to approach the Russians for additional firepower."

The first northern commander responded, "This idea is not as crazy as you might think. The Russians have long been a part of NATO. Back in 2002, the NATO-Russia Counsel was designed to allow Russia and European NATO to work together. The Counsel was down played by all parties and there were difficulties along the way... However, Russia has stated that they desire that someday they would be a full member in the alliance..."

At this point in the meeting, a third commander stood up. The other commanders turned and focused on him.

The third commander spoke up, "The subject of America's demise has already been discussed with the Russians and they concur, and are actually waiting for NATO. The Russians have been open to the idea for years. The plans and targets have already been formulated. And Sir... If you give the word, the final details and schedule will come easily. America will be made totally defenseless. There is only one caveat... With Israel's ally gone, Russia wants the honor of eliminating Israel herself. They have desired to do this since the 60's."[43]

Pul, stood up, lifted his glass and remarked, "Consider it done!"

CHAPTER ELEVEN

Come out of her my people

Back in Washington D.C., the news crew gathered in Sean's apartment. They were sitting around the TV.

Breaking news from TV announced, "Egypt beyond saving, total destruction..."

Sally gulped, "This can't be happening...massive destruction, endless suffering?" She's stunned. "I don't know what to say." The others were at different levels of shock.

Isaac voiced, "This just flies against everything I've ever believed... Another nation destroyed... How could it happen? What were they thinking? The world has gone crazy!"

Gus added "Statues and their hidden meaning aside, I have to put my foot down on this one. A bunch of coincidences can't make some prophecy mumbo jumbo a fact!"

Evelyn surprised at Gus, said, "Do you realize that this was done by the Assyrian! With his ten commanders! And the trigger was the Suez Canal! And the destruction was from Syene to Ethiopia just like the prophecy? The military analysts on the TV even estimates that it will be at least forty years till anyone can live there. You call that coincidence?"

Laura interrupted, "Stop! We're a news team let's act like it... Let's go with facts then. The American public still have no idea about Pul, but we know that he's consulting with NATO Europe about the U.S. problem. This will be a non-story for our agency."

Evelyn responded, "Exactly, but we have the prophecy which explains what Pul is doing and why!"

Isaac added, "We still haven't told anyone else what we know or where it comes from. Let's warn the government then! The pentagon! Anyone!"

Sally chimed in, "What about our jobs? I'm starting to lean towards these prophecies but we can't just leave our families, our friends, our lives here."

"You want to hop on a plane and get out of the country? Be my guest!" Gus exclaimed.

"All right! Enough! I know we're in a predicament right now but bickering isn't going to help. If the prophecies are true, we need to leave... And we need to do it right away. Let's all agree to go home tonight. Think about it. Talk to your families or whoever. Sleep on it. Report your personal decision in the morning." Sean snapped.

The next morning, at the crew's work break, they went across the street to the park. There was heavy silence between them.

Sean breaks the silence and spoke, "I talked to my dad, and he told me that since Aunt Kathy died last year, I'm now the family wacko. Then he asked if it was me he saw downtown last week with the signs over his head, 'REPENT THE END IS NEAR'. My mom just said that if you go, I should call her when I get back."

Laura gave a thin smile. "My sister told me the same thing, just not in so many words. I just tried to put myself in her place, I don't blame her. She just kept saying, that she doesn't believe me." Then she asked, "Gus, did you talk to your ex?"

"Yeah, she asked me if she would ever see me again. I said, probably not. She told me to go for it. And I told her that I still care."

Evelyn looked at them amazed, "Did you guys really think that your families would give up their lives, jobs, houses, cars to follow you to some other country, just because you've been reading books?! They've not gone through the same process we have, you know, since Oklahoma! We all know that we can't force them to come. But perhaps we can do better later. For right now it's an unreal expectation."

Isaac spoke quietly, "Before anyone else says anything, please hear me out. I had a dream last night."

Everyone looked at Isaac and waited for him to speak up.

Isaac recounted his dream, "An angel approached me. He pointed to a chalk board on the wall. A scripture reference written on it. Genesis 19:15 and the word "Australia" next to it." He continued, "I looked it up and the scripture said, 'and when the morning arose, then the angels hastened Lot, saying, arise take thy family which are here; lest thou be consumed in the iniquity of the city.'"

Isaac presented each member of the team a plane ticket. From D.C. to Sydney.

It will leave in fourteen hours. The others just looked at him.

Isaac continued, "Please, you're the only family I have... And besides, if I'm wrong then I'll look like a bloody idiot and you all get to have a free vacation, and we can come home and go back to work." No one says a word.

As their plane took off, they saw the city lights disappearing from their view.

After what seemed like an eternity, they finally landed in Sydney. They collected their baggage and equipment. No small task. It seemed they were carrying all the tools of their trade. Cameras, recorders, computers, communication gear and of course their clothes. As it is, they were dressed more like tourists ready to hit the beaches, than a news crew. They moved through the terminal. Something's off. Everyone in the terminal was congregated around the TV monitors in the concourse. No one was saying anything, just staring at the screen. Real time satellite images. It looked like volcanoes erupting. Laura went up to a nearby man.

"Excuse me, sir. Where is this happening?" inquired Laura.

The man flinched, as if back from a dream, and quipped. "America... those are cities... The whole bloody country is burning. East...West...Everything...The Russians launched a massive preemptive attack and the Americans had no defense... It was over in hours. Nothing was left but the smoke of her burning."

The news crew turned pale. They've heard that before from Revelations 18, *"They watch the smoke of her burning."* They knew now how close their escape had actually been.

They instinctively went to the nearest car rental and Sean drove them directly out of town as quickly as possible. No one said a word. They were in total shock and disbelief, but they all saw the fire and the destruction of America. They were too numb to talk. All communication was done with looks and nods. Finally, Sean pulled over and they gave in to the pain. Hours passed as they each tried to internalize and reconcile what had just happened. They tried to explain it away but it must be faced.

"We can never go home..." wept Sally.

Sean whispered, "There is no home. Everyone and everything's gone."

Laura sobbed, "What do we do now?"

Gus was silent.

CHAPTER TWELVE

The Russian Bear

Some Russian generals were huddled to see the aftermath of their attack. While others were discussing strategies.

"Now, for Israel..." began the first Russian general.

"But NATO guaranteed their security." The second general spoke.

"If that Assyrian gets in the way..." added the third general.

"We'll destroy him as well..." exclaimed the fourth general.

"He has agreed to stand back." A fifth general added.

At the same time In the Israeli command bunker, Israeli commanders and strategists were briefing a Knesset Leader, KP Levi Havie.

"It will take an act of God to be victorious..." KP Havie stated.

"We've been preparing for this battle since the 70's. We will not go down without a fight..." exclaimed the general.

The general handed Havie a heavily marked map. It is a large valley in Israel.

The general informed, "It runs from just east of the Haifa area and south for thirty miles and is ten miles wide. It's the valley of Jezreel."

KP Havie, looked up and asked, "Isn't it also known as..."

The general looked over at him and confirmed, "Yes, it is the valley of Armageddon."[44][45] The general continued, "The valley is nearly all agricultural with very few settlements. The perfect massive kill zone. Mountains on the west side and hills on the east, beyond the hills is the Great Rift Valley. This prevents a lateral retreat." The general stopped for a moment, then proceeded slowly, "The Russians don't have to use this valley to travel south. They could come through using the Golan and hold the high ground."

"How do we insure that they will use Jezreel?" KP Havie questions.

"We can't. However, we have made Jezreel look militarily soft. The path of least resistance. Here, after evacuating the locals, we'll spring operation BEAR TRAP. A group of tactical nuclear weapons have been planted in strategic locations throughout the valley...

Then a second nearly simultaneous attack using focused neutron technology." The general explained.

"Are you serious?! Neutron weapons were dismantled by the U.S. in 2003." KP Havie exclaimed.

The general explained further, "This battle cannot be lost... It's not a game, our very survival depends on how well we kill the enemy. Neutrons will be used precisely because they are lethal. We don't believe that the Russians will consider that Israel will use Nukes and Neutron weapons within her own borders. But if and when the time comes, we will."

KP Havie asked, "Won't destroying the attacking Russian forces bring Moscow's full wrath down on us? The Russian ICBM's would be used quickly?"

"yes" said the general, "But this is where OPERATION BIG BROTHER comes in to play."

"America?! She's dead. She couldn't save herself, how can she save us?" KP Havie asked.

The general continues, "American presets. They aren't directly tied to the United States government. The weapon systems, their deployment, targeting... They've been dispersed strategically around the world for years. Everything is preset.

The signal would commence automatically. Forty-five minutes prior to Bear Trap, a signal will be sent to release an attack on the Russian heartland. It's not necessary for America to exist to pull the trigger. We will do it. This is operation BIG BROTHER and NATO was never apprized. They don't know it is coming."

Within hours of America's destruction massive Russian forces mobilized and came south. And just as desired, they took the valley of Jezreel. Troops under close air support and aircrafts clogged the airspace. The battle field was swarmed with tanks, artillery and military vehicles. A typical overwhelming Russian offensive. They travelled from north to south and reached a point near the southern end of the valley.

The Israelis were monitoring the advance closely. As soon as the Russians reached a predetermined trip point in the south part of the valley, a command was issued, *"Qardom"* which means *"to strike like an axe"* in Hebrew.

Nuclear weapons blasted — Low yield, controllable—and in series—fire and flesh! A second nearly simultaneous attack. Neutron weapons were deployed overhead. They kill without impact. Russian air craft were suddenly with dead pilots. Tanks without live crews. Anyone that had survived the first round of tactical nukes were finished by the neutrons.

CHAPTER THIRTEEN

Armageddon

The news crew gathered in one of the rooms. Heavy static. A report on American survivors was interrupted.

"Israel attacks! Russia loses nearly 80% of the population in its western parts. No one understands how Israel could project so much power. But, not before the Russians decimated northern Israel, although there are those who think it was the Russians who were decimated in northern Israel. By an Israeli operation called 'BEAR TRAP' more aft-."

Sean, turned off the TV. Sally stared out the window. A small quiet town.

"How could little Israel defeat Russia?" Sean asked.

Sally responded, "The Lord says, 'I will put hooks into Russia's jaws and drag her into northern Israel to destroy her.' It will take seven months to bury the Russian dead in Israel and seven years to clean the site and remove all the weapons..." [46]

Evelyn bolted across the room and grabbed the book from a bag. "Daniel's seventieth week." she said.

They looked at her confused. She flipped to the bookmarked pages.

Evelyn reads, "It is a prophecy about the final seven years of the current age and it will precede the one thousand years of world peace. The events of this last seven years are also often referred to by the prophets as the 'Day of the Lord' or 'The time of God's wrath'. These seven years will start when Israel makes a seven year security agreement with the Assyrian."[47]

Laura asked, "Do you mean Pul's NATO security agreement started the clock for Daniel's seventieth week?"[48]

Evelyn confirmed, "Yes, within this week of years, seven military campaigns will take place which are actually associated with Pul. They are called collectively 'The Battles of Armageddon.'"

Confused, Isaac requested a clarification, "Can someone please tell me what's going on... In English please."

Gus explained, "Armageddon is not just one big battle as so many believe but rather a series." [49]

"Exactly!" Evelyn agreed.

"The first battle is the king of the south, Egypt... completely destroyed by fire from Libya to Ethiopia. It will be uninhabitable for forty years. The second battle is the 'King of the North', Gog of Magog, Russia, with the associated American destruction." Gus explained further.

Sean asked, "So, what's next?"

Evelyn replied, "The third campaign of military action is NATO moving from Western Europe into all of Eastern Europe and the parts of Asia not destroyed...

And then... The next campaign... Pul, the Assyrian... Moves into the Holy land...

and Jerusalem..." [50]

In Pul's spirit office, he pondered about the world events. Father Ibrahim sat across from him.

Father Ibrahim spoke, "Titans fall one after the other. You've exceeded my expectations."

Pul answers, "I have no love for Russia. The idea that they're gone, destroyed, that's just fine with me. This means one less competitor for control in the Middle East."

"And perhaps the whole world?" Father Ibrahim added.

"Yes" Pul states, "The world is getting smaller all the time and my ambitions are growing bigger."

Father Ibrahim smiled and said, "Was I called here for a confession? Tell me something I don't already know."

"Yes, of course. You see father, something is going on inside me. I have noticed that Asshur, the great God Asshur has been making mistakes." Pul stated. This gets a knowing look from the priest. Pul continued, "No need to worry. I've made sure that this will only be between us." From above them, a mystical barrier becomes visible.

"How do you do that?" the priest inquired.

"At times Asshur had no idea what I was thinking. Don't get me wrong, I still honor him with my substance... Money... but I reasoned within myself. What need of gold and silver does God have?" Pul remarked. [51]

Father Ibrahim concurred, "I have to admit from time to time he seems confused and disoriented. Asshur never lets on that anything was wrong. He would just cover mistakes by more bluster and accusations. There's always someone to blame."

"I recognize that Asshur is a powerful angelic being and should be appeased whenever possible but..." Pul added.

Father Ibrahim interrupted, "But you no longer see him as god?"

Pul laughed hard. "Actually, I have more trust in your powers and counsel, father..." Father Ibrahim knelt before Pul.

CHAPTER FOURTEEN

Time to Flee Jerusalem

Photographers, journalists and writers were imbedded in Pul's forces to chronicle events that will take place. Pul and his troops moved in columns to Jeba, a small village just north of Jerusalem. [52] Their approach was gentle and methodical. The locals greeted them with suspicion. Pul came down from his armored jeep to address the gathering crowd in the town square.

Pul addressed them, "People of Jeba, in accordance with the security agreement, we have come here as your allies. I hope that by the evening you will be our kind hosts and that tomorrow we will repay you generously."

A polite applause. The town's leader embraced Pul. Pul looked on as his troops interacted with the locals. Some played with the children. Pul thinks, *like a cat with a mouse*. Under the cover of darkness. More of Pul's troops moved from the north. Jerusalem was now surrounded.

In the morning, Pul's forces deployed against Jerusalem. Shrieks pierced the morning. Guns fire. Bullet casings dropped into a pool of blood. For those who were still in Jerusalem, it was too late for them to run.

Pul himself entered through the Mount Scopus area, the old city of Nob. He stopped long enough to lift his fist against the city and decreed, "I am the king."

Photographers, journalists and writers took note of the event. Writers jot down what Pul said. Lights flashed from different angles coming from the photographer's cameras. [53]

The Jewish priests and ministers were in the temple in fervent prayer. Bang! Doors flew open. Pul entered with a piece of paper in his hand. His men flooded behind him. They arrested and removed all of the Jewish priests, except for one. His men dragged the chief priest before Pul.

Pul looked at the paper. It's a list. Names of religious leaders, political big shots and high ranking military officers. Most of their names were already crossed out. They lifted the priest's horrified face. Pul crossed off another name. The soldiers shot the priest near the altar of sacrifice in the court yard.

Father Ibrahim came up behind Pul and whispered, "I know some other names you can add..."

"Be my guest." Pul replied.

Father Ibrahim explained, "The locals refer to them as 'The Prophets'. For three and a half years, they've been preaching that Jesus is the Messiah."[54]

In the heart of old Jerusalem, the two prophets were preaching in the middle of a gathered crowd. The people around them started mocking and provoking them. Still, they continued preaching.

One of them said, "Sinners, repent!"

The other one said, "You should have fled Jerusalem when you saw the armies surrounding the city!"[55]

"Why should I waste bullets on these two?" Pul asked.

Father Ibrahim explained, "Because these prophets have power in their words. A couple of officers came to arrest the men. They called down fire on them from heaven. And not from NATO like you did in Egypt... The officers were consumed on the spot. The police in the city have given up trying to arrest them."

Pul seemed unconcerned. He got on his field phone and sent a team of snipers into the old city.

"Track down the men they call 'the prophets. Kill them on the spot. Don't get close to them. Let them lie where they fall. Let everyone see it." commanded Pul.

The snipers did their job. The two men are laid out on the streets. Each shot through the heart. The people around the bodies rejoiced and mocked them. [56]

Three years ago, a group of Jewish and Christian men became aware from scripture that they needed to begin to prepare for a time called *Jacob's trouble* and what the Christians called *the Great tribulation*.[57][58] They knew that the people in Judea would need to flee into the mountains for refuge. These men began a covert operation to fill some caves and tunnels, in Edom, a place South East of the Dead Sea, in Jordan, with food, water and all the necessities of life. This would be for three and one half years. This exodus would be triggered by Pul's invading forces into Jerusalem.

Yoram, the leader of the operation to prepare the wilderness stronghold set a meeting in a stone home just south of Jerusalem. The home was guarded by a group of men wearing traditional Arab garb, with their weapons hidden under them. The men were Jewish but didn't want to attract attention. A man entered the house.

"What do we have?" inquired Yoram.

"Pul and his forces are in Michmash, a small town ten miles north." The man replied.

Yoram nodded. The man presented a map to Yoram and said, "We've only got days till we leave."

Yoram unfolded the map and placed it on the table. Yoram produced a book of his own which had a map folded within it. He quickly compared the maps.

"We have a match" he said. "The paths are confirmed, Pul's and ours. He'll be stopping in Jeba tomorrow night. We will leave tonight to the south, and we won't stop until we are safely in the stronghold. Remember this exodus must be covert, cover your lights and move slowly. Don't create dust or noise." Yoram ordered.

The man nodded his head and asked, "How many are there?"

"Just the Jews alone will be in excess of 144 thousand." Yoram replied. [59].

They all began to thank God for his mercy and direction.

The next night, Pul is in Jeba, waiting for the next day.

Yoram and the people were now in the ancient city of Petra.[60] They entered the long abandoned Nabataean city through the entrance which was a mile long split in the rock walls.

Yoram entered the great vaults of the stock room. He looked absolutely minuscule compared to the city's caches of food and water that were meant to last them an entire three and a half years.

CHAPTER FIFTEEN

Pul, King of Jerusalem

Pul was looking out on the city, his city, on a palatial balcony. One of his generals was beside him, reporting something. Pul burst out laughing.

"So that's where they are. They're hiding under a rock?" laughed Pul.

The general responded, "We'll be prepared to eliminate them all tomorrow—"

"No!" Pul said emphatically.

General asked, "Sir?"

"No, don't kill them straight away. They're not going anywhere. They'll be hungry and thirsty in a short time... Then we can destroy them anytime we wish." Pul stated.

The Temple mount only days later. All the Muslim structures were being demolished.

"I have a lot to do in Jerusalem... My world capital..." Pul boasted.

Pul's men also moved into the west bank areas of the Palestinians. His men roughed up and disarmed a Palestinian police officer.

"I have no tolerance for Islam of any form. They are dangerous to me." Pul said.

In Gaza, Hamas' stronghold, a man was pleading into a news camera in tears. "The Palestinian nation is completely dissolved! It is no more!"[61]

A SKY News reporter was with an irate political activist. He reported, "Hamas and others thought that the fall of Jerusalem was good news for them. Their enemy, Israel, fallen."

The activist cried, "That illusion was short lived. Pul turned on us! The crusaders have returned."

"And the Israeli government is being treated just as poorly." responded the reporter.

Back at the Jewish temple, Father Ibrahim entered the temple. Pul's men followed behind. They proceeded to remove the furniture, altars, tables and curtains. They were all dumped outside. Father Ibrahim commanded that the implements for handling the sacrifices were to remain in place. The priest walked towards a pig carcass.

"Perfect, we will use this pig as the last sacrifice to Jehovah. A fitting sacrament to a defeated God." the priest stated. [62] He continued to redecorate the temple's holy place. He placed Pul's image in the front and center of the sanctuary and a smaller symbol of the Assyrian god Asshur to his right hand.

Back in the old city. The corpses of the two prophets began to move after three days and they stood to their feet. They are alive!

And a loud voice came thundering from above, it spoke, "Come up here!"

The two prophets began to rise into the air. They both rose till they disappeared into a cloud. [63]

The people watching the event were too stunned to speak. Then, the fear hit them. A woman fled the area as quickly as she could. The woman, looking very upset, reported what she saw to Father Ibrahim. The woman was now hysterical as she's relaying what she saw.

"An illusion. A trick to scare the public." The priest's voice was heavily irritated.

"I know what I saw!" the woman exclaimed.

"Of course you do" the priest agreed and walked away from her and towards the large statue of Pul in the temple. He looked up in admiration. The response had been remarkable. Virtually, everyone that went through the ceremony bowed and worshipped the image of Pul. [64] He found the marking ceremonies being interrupted. He hears a young woman shouting.

"Stop! Stop!" shouted the young woman.

The priest found the guards pointing their guns at an old man on the floor.

"Papa, please do it! Just bow and swear allegiance! Please!" pleaded the young woman.

He spit at the statue, and cried, "Jerusalem is spiritually unclean like Sodom..." [65]

A gun blast was heard faintly from outside.

Back inside the temple, a small child and her mother were waiting in line to get their markings.

"When someone completes the ceremony, he or she is given a mark in their skin to indicate citizenship in the new world order..." the mother stated.

The child responded, "I want that one, Mama." She pointed to a teenager with an Assyrian Star marked on her forehead.

"No... That's the lowest level, dear. The second level is the king's name written in Aramaic and the third is his name written in the number 666. That's what we want to get." the mother added. [66]

"Will it hurt?" the child asked.

"No, it doesn't seem to, besides, without having one of these marks in your skin... you can't buy or sell anything. We would be locked out of society. We don't have much choice." Explained the mother.

The child exclaimed, "Mama, look!" The child pointed at Pul's statue,

The Demons were making the image talk and look alive. The people who came to worship were amazed by the image. They did not understand how it was happening. [67] Father Ibrahim flashed a stern look at the demons, to keep them in line. Since the removal of the Christians, they felt much freer to manifest themselves.

Pul and Father Ibrahim were meeting in Pul's spirit office to discuss some disturbing spiritual developments on the earth. When Asshur made his traditional light show entrance, this time, he had no angelic consorts. He folded his wings and stood facing Pul and Father Ibrahim beside the desk. They looked more irritated than impressed.

Asshur spoke, "I'm pleased to see that you two found space in the temple for my symbol. However small it is..."

Asshur was clearly angry and staring directly at Father Ibrahim.

Pul spoke up, "I felt it was the least we could do. After all, it's not every day that a fallen angel is honored in the Jewish temple."[68]

Asshur was surprised by Pul's insolence but did not lose his temper. "So...

You're sticking up for each other. I suppose that's good. But you two really are full of yourselves. You could get in trouble." Asshur hesitated. He looked to the side and then back at Pul.

Pul did not hesitate. "I have honored you with my wealth and given my time to you. I am grateful that you helped us establish Assyria again. However, I will not worship you. You are not a god. You are an angel. A mighty angel to be sure but not a god. I intend to show to you and Jehovah that I am the god of this world." [69]

Father Ibrahim looked at Pul in disbelief, not because of what he said, but he was amazed that Pul could actually say those things to Asshur. He dropped his head, expecting Asshur to explode. But to his surprise he didn't. He held his anger and began to explain himself.

"Yes, I am a fallen angel and my name is 'Heylel' or Lucifer. I am at war with Jehovah Elohim. I served the God of heaven until I questioned his very nature. He claims to be self-existent. The 'I am that I am'. I don't believe that he is omnipotent or omnipresent. Jehovah has predicted the outcome of these current events..." Asshur stated. [70]

Pul interrupted Asshur. "There are literally millions of angels on and around the earth right now. Who are they?" Pul asked. [71]

Asshur responded, "They are the fallen angels from heaven which supported me at my trial. They are fighting to hold the earth."

Pul interrupted Asshur again. "Your angels are in full retreat! You expect them to stop God's anointed angels?"

Asshur, now speaking in full anger, "I am preparing to lead this world and everyone in it for the final battle. Pul, you, Father Ibrahim, and your armies belong to me! I also command several armies of Nephilim which are hidden and waiting to join the battle. If I fail... you will fail, too. Judgment by fire."[72]

Asshur left in a flash of light. Pul and Father Ibrahim took a deep breath and returned to their meeting.

"Have you instituted the marking program on the global level?" Pul asked Father Ibrahim.

"Yes, but the kings of the east... China and others are mustering a massive army and are marching this way. We've even received notice that three of our European allies are refusing to cooperate. Three of the ten!" Father Ibrahim replied. [73][74]

Pul instructs, "Go out to the Euphrates and make a kill zone along the river. [75] Use all the weapons you need to utterly annihilate them. It's time to cull the herd. They cannot be allowed to cross the river! If our allies in Europe still feel rebellious after they see this, then destroy their capitals. Reduce them to rubble. Tear them up by the roots!" Pul continued, "By the way, remember my new stronghold in Jerusalem, get it built." [76]

CHAPTER SIXTEEN

We Need to Get Out of Here

The DC news crew moved to a location on the outskirts of Darwin in northern Australia. A small but suitable house. The news crew was busy. Evelyn was operating the short wave radios. Most of the high tech satellite networks were not working. But the more basic nations have turned back to using short wave radio. Evelyn, being a communications expert built the radio set up. A faint voice came out of her headset. It was with an Indonesian accent and broken English. She jotted the message down on a sheet, ripped it off, and gave it to Sally. Laura read it and passed it to Gus. He pinned the note strategically on a huge cork board. Gus stepped back. The cork board was filled with a startling number of charts, references, clippings and data.

"The systematic destruction of nations is tracking just like the book of Daniel lays it out." Gus stated.

Laura came over with the book. She read, "The mark of the beast which is instituted by the false prophet will be forced on everyone on the earth in the next few months. [77] The army comes to earth from heaven to destroy the beast's kingdom and everyone which has his mark."

Everyone was now on the couch facing the wall of data. Isaac looked at Sean with a questioning look.

Sean stated, "Joel's army is a term for God's army which is described in the book of Joel. This is the army that destroys the armies of the nations and their cities, anyone with Pul's mark. It says if those in Joel's army fall on a sword while fighting it will not hurt them."[78]

"The only safe people in the world are in Edom. I'm not even sure where Edom is exactly, but our prophecy charts say that the Jews are there. Those who fled from Judea." Sally spoke.

"Great. We need to get out of here. Let's make a run for it." Isaac impatiently said.

"Not so fast" Sean pointed out, "We have four hurdles to overcome. Lack of funding is the first."

"Right now we have enough money for a simple life here in Australia for a few years but not for bribes and clandestine passage on ships. We can't just buy a ticket on an airplane to Edom."

Sean added "Second, we can't just show up at Petra without bringing supplies."

"I feel the same way. We need to buy our way into the stronghold once we get there... if we can get there at all." Gus said.

Sean continued, "Third, we must secure sea passage of some sort from Australia to Saudi Arabia and then land passage to Petra."

Isaac asked, "And the fourth is?"

Sean answered, "We must do it all without anyone in authority finding out."

Three days later, on the porch of the house. Isaac was looking far off. Sally sat down to join him.

"Is that angel still on your mind?" Sally asked.

Isaac ignored her question and went straight to his own question. "I don't know why God warned us back in DC. We aren't Christians or seeking God in any way, Sally. So, does God want us to do something? If so, what?"

"All I know is we're on the clock. We'll need to make a move soon..." replied Sally.

Isaac said quietly, "My brother called this morning. He told me that my father had died and that there is a distribution of the inheritance. The good news is that there's a lot of chaos in the world and money is being moved all around to keep it safe. It's helpful that Australia is also a part of the British Commonwealth." Isaac hesitated, "You know we've seen so much death and destruction you would think this news about my dad wouldn't bother me... But it really has hit me hard..."

Sally gave Isaac a hug. As he begin to cry.

Then he took a deep breath and turned to Sally. "It's in excess of £300,000. It'll fund our excursion with no problem. We just have to split it up... Make the expenditures harder to follow and cover our backs."

The crew piled into a small white work van. One of two that Isaac leased for the project. They drove around Darwin, dropping one of the crew at each bank. They set up accounts at each location with their name and another member can sign as well. They went to bulk food warehouses and grocery stores in the area to buy food and water. They were grateful that the area still had plenty of food. Much of the world had gone to rationing in anticipation of food shortages. Actually, it turned out to be harder finding large amounts of containerized purified water than food.

"We can't let on that we're helping Jews in the Middle East, but we'll have to find others to help if we're ever going to leave Darwin." Sean stated.

"We have friends in Saudi Arabia that urgently need humanitarian help. It breaks my heart..." Gus spoke.

"I think we can sell that..." Sean remarked.

In an isle of a small local grocery. Sean was wheeling his cart, it's about full.

He stopped. The shelf was quite picked over. He took all the packs of salt there.

At the checkout counter, the cashier excused himself and went to the back room. Sean's hand was shaking. When the grocer returned to the counter, he looked at Sean in the eye.

"Son, you've been here four times this week..." stated the grocer.

Sean was ready to bolt.

The grocer continued, "We can save a lot of time if you just tell me how much you really need."

"Ten tons?" The grocer just smiled. "Remember me when the time comes.

Where do you want it delivered?" asked the grocer.

The crew moved from their house to more suitable accommodations. Sean unlocked the door to a small warehouse near the water and entered. They've amassed an impressive number of rations. The rest of the crew were busy labeling, repacking and taking account of the stock.

He went straight up a stairway which led to an upper room, turned into a Spartan living space. Beds, bags, clothes, a small cooker, and other necessities. He went to Evelyn who is at her desk, still listening on the two-way ham radio. She took off the head phones.

"I hate to break it to you, Sean. No one in Australia wants to go to Saudi Arabia or anywhere else in the Middle East... For any amount of money."

Sean was clearly stressed running his fingers through his hair, "I guess we'll find another way."

The team met later that evening in the upper room. They all sit around the table.

Sean began, "I asked myself, why would God help us to this point and then not show us the way? Then it hit me. We haven't really exhausted all our options."

Evelyn perplexed, "I've called everyone on your list, Sean. What do you mean?"

Sean began to make the sign of the cross. "This is one thing none of us had ever done or believed in…"

The rest started to follow awkwardly. Laura held Sean's hand. Sean held Isaac's hand and so on. Together they bowed their heads.

Sean spoke, "Uhm… God… We acknowledge what you have done for us… We thank you. We acknowledge that we have been unbelievers but now we need your help. We now believe you are real. You are our only hope. Please, please forgive us."

They each said Amen one after the other then-- SQUAK. They all looked at the two-way ham radio.

"Americans… Americans, who need ship to Saudi?" the voice from the radio asked. The crew skeptically looked at each other.

Laura asked, "Captain Darma? Is that you?"

"Yes" the man from the other line echoed back.

"How did he know?" asked Isaac.

"This might be a trap or something." Gus whispered.

Evelyn rushed back to her desk and spoke to the radio, "Darma, Evelyn here… What? Say that again?" Then she switched to her headphones as the reception was poor. "Say that again? Uh-huh, oh." She turned to the crew. "The Australian captains talked with the Indonesian captains. Word had gotten out that some Americans needed passage to Saudi Arabia and that they have money. He called us because we are the only Americans, he knew... Should we make arrangements?" she asked them.

"Let me talk to him." Sean responded.

"Hold on. Talking about this on the radio could give away our plans." Gus interrupted.

"Gus, we just prayed for help. We'll just have to trust that no one listening will turn us in." He sat down on the desk and pulled out Thomas's pen. It became Sean's favorite pen now, and he got some paper ready. Evelyn handed him the headphones.

"Darma, this is Sean. We need your ship to be in Darwin in one week. Will you be able to do that?" Sean spoke to the radio.

The captain responded, "Yes, yes. Of course, I do it, no problem."

"Will it be able to carry 50 tons of palleted cargo and five passengers to Saudi Arabia in as direct a path as possible?" asked Sean.

The captain answered, "Yes, yes. Australia no allow harbor. But fake engine emergency allows." Then he laughs.

"What did he say?" asked Gus.

Sean looked at his notes. "He's done this before. The loading of the cargo would have to be done with cooperation from the Australian dock workers. The right money to the right people. He calls it overtime pay. He'll make all the arrangements."

After an overstressed week of wondering who was going to knock on the door, the ship arrived right on schedule. The news crew was surprised to find a fishing boat. The crew had expected a freighter.

Isaac asked confused, "I thought he had a freighter, that's a bloody fishing boat!"

Sean chimed in, "At least it's reasonably large..."

They both looked up and saw the boat's crew waving at them from the deck. The ship was a big hunk of metal, fading paint, and rust four large booms for loading and unloading fish from the holds.

"I hope it's seaworthy." Sean remarked.

"I'm sure it is... we prayed for this, didn't we?" Isaac said.

As the news crew walked to the boat. Gus was having a hard time keeping a straight face.

"We prayed for this? We should be more specific with our prayers. The cargo's going to smell like fish by the time we arrive in the Middle East!"

On board the ship, Captain Darma, a small Thai man in his 50's with a big smile shook hands with the news crew.

"The repairs made quickly." He winked at them twice. "We leave port right on time." He turned to his crew, laughed and shouted some orders in Thai as he walked.

The ship sailed north to East Timor. The ship was actually much faster than her appearance belied. They stopped to take on fuel, both in the ship's tanks and some auxiliary tanks which were for use on longer voyages. The stop was strictly business and no one went ashore. The news crew never even went to the deck, they didn't want to be seen by anyone. They quickly resumed the trip on to their next port of call, which was Jakarta. After some negotiation, the boat crew was allowed some shore time since this was their home port, and they have family there. But they could not discuss their destination, cargo or passengers with anyone at all. And again, the Americans stayed below deck, this was no vacation. The ship left port right on time the next morning with the understanding that the next stop would be their destination. They plotted a course several hundred miles south of India. This was an attempt to avoid any entanglements in India's affairs. India had been devastated just years earlier by the comet collision, and was still grappling to survive. As the trip continued in earnest, the news crew felt for the first time since they left home that they can decompress mentally. After all there's little they can do right now but wait. Of course, Evelyn still worked like crazy to get more communication links and news about the world, especially from the Middle East.

By and large, this was a fruitless endeavor, but it passed the time.

As they began to get closer to Saudi Arabia, the anxiety level began to ramp up. They knew that they need to inform the captain of their true destination which was Aqaba Jordan and not Saudi.

Sean watched the crew and sailors having a good time sharing stories, and playing cards.

"It's a shame we have to tell him. Because he and his crew are having the cruise of their lives. They're really along for the ride. They're fishermen without having to fish! They'll still get paid." Sean stated.

The day came. In the captain's cabin, Captain Darma was screaming something in Thai. Laura, Sean and Gus were not sure what to do or say.

"I know we don't have contacts at Aqaba, but I hope..." Laura spoke.

The captain cut Laura's speech, "You lie to me! You lie!" He exploded. "I stop at Mecca! You remove cargo and leave! Leave!" he screamed.

Laura begged, "Please understand, it would be safer for you and your crew if they showed up in Jordan with humanitarian supplies than Mecca."

"Right, Jordan has suffered real hardships since Amman has been destroyed." Sean added.

The captain was still not appeased. Gus came forward and grabbed the captain's hand.

"Something extra... For your trouble." Gus said as he handed the captain extra cash.

The captain looked at the large wad of cash in his hand. He started laughing and shaking their hands. He shouted directions at his crew in Thai. He then ran a course up the Gulf of Aqaba in the night. No small feat. As the sun came up, the anchor was lowered. They arrived just outside the port. The news crew were busy preparing their things for departure when a small boat filled with men in traditional Arab garb came to the ship. Each of them looked intimidating. The crew brought the men on board. The leader of the men spoke to Captain Darma in perfect Thai.

"Take us to the American reporters." The leader ordered.

The news crew all looked worried and unsure of what's happening as the men escorted them to the ship's galley. The leader of the men motioned for the sailors there to leave immediately. The leader spoke to the news crew, in perfect English.

"We know who you are. We're here to help facilitate your mission to deliver the supplies to the stronghold. We've cleared you to dock at the port and arrangements have been made to unload and reload the cargo into trucks which are currently waiting for you." said the leader of the men in Arab garb.

Sean asked, "Who are you?"

The leader simply put his hands up in front of his face. "Not now." he replied and asked Sean, "How much cargo did you bring?"

Sean replied, "Fifty tons, including water."

The leader looked at them all and smiled. "Well done."

Meanwhile at the port, a number of men were loading the cargo into large trucks. The news crew were directed to climb into some jeeps. Soon, the entire caravan headed out of Aqaba and drove up the rift road inside the Jordanian border travelling to the north. The stronghold was fifty miles north and about ten miles east.

The ride was somewhat bumpy but still most of the crew managed to sleep.

Laura was leaning on Gus' shoulder. Both had weary faces.

Sally asked, "Is this really happening? Do you think they'll let us in?"

"I don't know? I'm just as nervous as you, kid." Gus replied.

CHAPTER SEVENTEEN

Petra

Laura looked out the window. She saw a series of buildings in the desert just in front of the rock faces. These used to be the tourist information centers and restaurants. They're all emptied and locked up now.

Sean was awaken by the commotion. The other members were poking their heads out the window. The trucks approached the opening of the high-walled crack in the rock which was the winding entrance to Petra. The trucks were greeted by men in military uniforms. Other men were starting to transfer the supplies from the large transport trucks to small pickup trucks and trailers to convey the supplies inside. The news crew were also helping out. The Arab garbed men from the ship earlier approached them.

"You've done your share for today. Come with us. There is someone who wants to speak with you." The crew followed them.

As they entered the stronghold, their mouths gape in awe. The grand sandstone façade of Petra: Roman-style pillars, alcoves and plinths were carved masterfully into the rock face. Further inside the complex, the crew were greeted by hugs and applauses from a sizeable crowd.

Gus whispered to himself, "I could get used to this."

A man in his 60's approached the crew and shook their hands. "It's wonderful to finally meet you all! I am Yoram, the leader here in Petra."

Sean introduced himself, "My name is Sean. We're a news—"

Yoram interrupted, "We all know who you are..."

"But, how? There are no communications in or out of here. The satellites are all down." Sean asked.

"Over one hundred thousand people in the stronghold prayed that God would bring them what they need. We pray to the heavens, but not to Satellites. Our communications are in the spirit." explained Yoram.

"What did you mean, need?" Sean asked again.

"The calculations had been done concerning Petra's food and water supplies. We found that a shortage would occur in the last three weeks of the siege... And your crew answered the call!" Yoram added.

The crew were all genuinely surprised and stunned.

Laura asked in a whisper, "Sir, does this mean we can stay here with you?"

Yoram looked at Laura directly. "Yes of course. You're safe now..."

Laura can't hold it any longer. She dropped to her knees with tears streaming down her face.

"Thank you." She said.

The other members jumped to her aid and held her. By this time, they were all in tears.

After they got their composure, Yoram took the crew around the stronghold.

Yoram explained, "It is very important that order and discipline be maintained. Spending years in confinement is not an easy existence. Everyone must share in the work. No one can allow themselves to get bored or depressed. Even though we have only weeks remaining."

He showed them the mundane activities in Petra. Child care, guards being changed and removal of trash. They also got to see the spiritual side of the activities. They saw people congregating to the main court where there were twelve large and distinct tribes. They worshipped, sang, and studied the Bible.

At evening, Yoram took them to the mess tents where the people took their meals. The crew were sitting around a covered lantern. The cover on the lantern prevented the light from going up in the sky. It was a security precaution. Isaac finished his dinner and when the rest of the crew were done and they all were admiring the stars overhead.

CHAPTER EIGHTEEN

The Angels

The men who boarded their ship that morning came to join them. Isaac saw one of them. A face he can't pinpoint. While the crew engaged with them, the man sat beside Isaac.

Isaac asked him, "Excuse me, but have we met before? You seem very familiar."

The man asked him back, "You don't recognize me?"

Isaac really looked at his face, then he gasped. "You're the angel from my dream!"

The others turned their attention to them.

Isaac continued, "How is it possible? You look somehow different..."

"I can change my appearance to suit my situation. You needed an angel with wings to convince you back in D.C. so you'd move quickly. But, on the ship you needed a man to direct you. Wings would never do. Most of the time I'm not even visible." The angel replied. [79]

It sank in to the others that they're in the midst of angels. A second man joined the conversation. He sat next to Sally. She looked at the angel beside her in awe.

"It's our biggest advantage to see and hear without detection. The ministry of the Ruwack Kodesh has changed since the resurrection of the believers." The angel explained. [80]

Isaac asked, "Who is the Ruwack Kodesh?"

The second angel answered, "The Holy Spirit. But while he no longer seeks a bride for the Elect One, whom you'd know as the man, Jesus Christ. We angels are busier than ever. The seventh and final battle is near. We are excited to see it. We've never seen the Elect One move in anger. We hope he does not remove everything."

"What do you mean everything?" asked Evelyn.

He smiled at their increasingly perplexed faces.

"The world is actually empty. By that I mean the world consists of atoms." He points to the lantern. Sally looks deep into the light. The angel creates a vision in the light and said, "The atoms themselves are 99.99% space inside."

The vision zoomed in to the atomic level. The crew saw the atoms as small balloons of energy, all touching each other.

The first angel continued, "The energy is what makes for the color and hardness you see as the world around you."

Another angel manipulated the vision within the light. The crew saw the blooming cosmos.

"God saw his creation and said it is good. If the energy holding the universe together were to vanish... The world would be gone." The other angel said.

The vision of the cosmos swirls violently and then pop, it disappeared.

The second angel added, "The Elect One, Jesus, is the source of that energy."

The crew was captivated by every word.

The second angel explained further, "Scripture says his weapon is the sword of his mouth with his words can remove energy, destroy or create it. It will be according to his will."[81]

A vision of spirits formed at the lantern.

"His enemies think they can manipulate matter through their spells and magic and compete with his power. They forgot that he holds them together. In him all things consist!" added the first angel.

The angel waved his hand and the spirits disappeared in a blink of an eye.

The first angel continued to speak, "Your race of humans is not very old. Your first father was a man called Adam. His DNA was perfect. His spirit was placed within his body by God at the time of his creation. He was of very high intellect. All this changed when he violated God's law. Adam's body became frail and sick.

He begins to age. His intellect degrades and he dies. All of these deficiencies in Adam's genetics were passed along to each generation of Adam's family."

The second angel added, "While mankind is still intelligent. You are still nothing like your father Adam was before the fall."

"But we've been taught that the Genesis account of creation was a myth." Sally spoke.

The third angel responded, "The Genesis account would seem simplistic to some men, but it is an accurate account. Although never intended to explain all the details of creation. It was made simple so no man could claim it was too complex for him to understand. The reason we're explaining the nature of man is so that you will understand that no one really dies– only the body dies. When you see the mass deaths on the earth, through wars and cataclysmic events, understand that these people don't cease to exist. They are actually relocated to Sheol, the place of the dead. It is a vast and dark cavern with many levels and compartments. Each one a holding cell for the spirits of the wicked dead."[82]

The first angel adds, "God will set up a kingdom that he will lead. The world's governments which now exist will be completely removed. This new kingdom is the one that every Christian has prayed for when they say the Lord's Prayer, 'thy

kingdom come, thy will be done on earth as it is in heaven.'"
The first angel added. [83]

Still, by the lantern side the angel continued, "When you
went to Oklahoma to search for the missing people, you could
not find them because they had been removed. It was necessary
that their bodies be changed before they could rise. They are
now like Adam, before the fall. They are now spiritual. They
now have eternal life...You will meet them shortly. They will be
with the Lord as his bride and part of his army."[84]

CHAPTER NINETEEN

Changing The Laws and Times

Back in Jerusalem, the city was now spiritually called Sodom and Egypt. After the removal of the two witnesses, the city had become truly unclean.

Pul was in the temple. He handed a piece of paper to Father Ibrahim.

"I'm giving orders for my changes to be instituted now that we've moved into the temple. It's a list." Pul said. [85]

Father Ibrahim started reading.

Pul continued, "I am determined to put our mark on the world. I'm tired of submitting to the rules and regulations which were put in place by Jehovah and his followers down through the ages."

As the priest was reading, he grew more perplexed. "Really?" he asked.

"Yes, really! And do it before the end of the seven year security agreement." Pul exclaimed.

Father Ibrahim nodded. He held the paper over his head and the paper disappeared as a hand pulls it into the spirit. A group of spirits were gathered just outside our reality. A ranking spirit, one bigger than the others, read the list. The lower spirits peeked over to get a look.

"What's it say? What's it say?" they asked.

The ranking spirit kept the paper to himself with an angry look. Then he began to smirk. The others were confused.

"From now on, the week will be six days long, and there will be five weeks per month..." the ranking spirit began to read aloud.

At first, the spirits just smirked. Then as they looked at each other, they can't hold it in. They explode in mocking laughter.

"What's next they demand?"

The spirit read, "No one shall observe the Sabbath in any way."

The rank spirit commented, "They outlawed the observance of the Sabbath. They aren't just going to place themselves up as gods to replace Jehovah, but actually establish laws that would eliminate Jehovah and all memory of him!"

The spirits guffawed. The ranking spirit continued reading, "All reference to the Jews and their Torah shall be removed from society. Destroy all religious books, documents and symbols from any and all religions."

One of the spirits snatched the list and he continued to read aloud. "The Assyrian base sixty numbering system shall replace the existing base ten system."

Another spirit stole the list. "The new calendar is to have three hundred and sixty days in a year. The additional..." He stopped as he was laughing too hard.

Another spirit stole the list. He said, "The additional five solar days in the year would be used to worship Pul!"

They continued, "The year would start at the summer solstice and the years would be counted as BP or AP. BP is Before Pul and AP is After Pul. The year one started when Pul entered Jerusalem."

"Wow... Pul is having a great time being god!" The ranking spirit exclaimed.

Suddenly, a disembodied voice shouted.

"Silence! Just get it done!" Father Ibrahim commanded.

The spirits flinched and disappeared.

CHAPTER TWENTY

Zedekiah's Grotto and Petra

Pul, Marodeen, Father Ibrahim and about twenty-five men were led to a cave and quarry by an engineer. The cave was just north of the temple complex and under the old city. It's called Zedekiah's Grotto. [86] The cave had a large steel blast door at the entrance. The engineer ushered the men past the door, and further into the heavy reinforced concrete cave.

Pul, positions himself in front of them. "Gentlemen, you are all my most important allies and essential people to my government. As such, you have earned a place here in our new stronghold in Zedekiah's Grotto." He said.

The men cheered. He turned and they followed him on in. Pul and his men explored the space. It was stark but had all the necessary amenities. An engineer came over to him.

"Is everything to your liking, sir?" whispered the engineer.

"Yes, you've done well. Now I want to see my own accommodations." Pul said.

"Yes of course." the engineer led him on.

Pul, in his own chamber, closed the door behind him. The fluorescent light above him flickered and then went pitch dark. His spiritual counselors gathered around him.

The first counselor began, "It has become clear...with time... That the Jews in Petra are not coming out on their own..."

Pul replies, "I want them gone before the seven year security agreement lapses. You have only weeks before that time. I have used all my neutron weapons against the kings of the east. A tactical nuke... might be dropped right into the center of Petra. But there's no guarantee that all the people would die from the initial blast... But they certainly would not survive the fall out..."

The spirits chuckled.

"Why are you all laughing?" Pul asked.

"We know how to do it. We've done it before! We had previously destroyed the Nabataeans who lived in Petra. That destruction took place around the fourth century A.D. It looked like a natural disaster but we did it!" The spirits said proudly. "We used an earthquake and flood. Spiritually triggered and naturally accomplished. We used the earthquake to loosen the rocks and sand within Petra... And then caused a massive rain storm over the city... Petra is essentially a large rock basin with a drain at one end. The drain is the narrow cut in the rocks leading out of the city. And our storm was greater than they had seen before and the channel out of the city clogged up with sand. The city went under fifty feet of water. Those who actually survived left the city and never returned."

Pul asked, "Can you do it again?"

"Yes, of course. The site has not changed at all since that time. If you send troops to Petra and seal the entrance, we can cause the rain and quake. The results should be the same." cheered the spirits.

"Very well. I give you my order." Pul responded.

The spirits dispersed and they can hardly contain they're excitement. Now in Petra, the spiritual powers hovered around the stronghold. They started to perform a dance-like ritual. It was quickly broken as God's angels pressed them further back from the stronghold. They cursed as they fall back. The spiritual powers hovered further back around Petra. The skies turned darker, more sinister. A small segment of the earth and sand parted. It went virtually unnoticed.

The people had been told by the angels to stay well above the valley floor. God's angels in Petra knew what was being attempted.

The Assyrian troops arrived at the entrance channel of Petra. They parted formation so that two cranes can pass through. They quickly put in place a series of stackable concrete blocks in front of the entrance.

A group of people were huddled together on the other side. Most of them are in fervent prayer. A woman calmed her young children.

"It's going to be all right." She hushes them.

The news crew scoured the plaza to find the angels. They found them at the watch tower and stood behind them, overseeing the progress of Pul's troops through the CCTV monitor.

The Angels saw the crew and explained, "We don't need to do anything about it... We are sealed within Petra."

Outside the entrance, the blockade was now thirty feet high. The entire structure was then covered with sprayed on, quick drying concrete. The people inside were busy preparing for the flood. They took all essential equipment, food, water and fuel to higher points in the sides of Petra. There was an obvious tension but the people were very disciplined and organized under the direction of the angels.

The ritual by the spiritual powers of Asshur became more intense. Their chants louder, their dance more frantic. Then they stopped. Silence. A glass of water shaked slightly. The people within Petra braced themselves. The spirits looked down, bewildered. They restarted their ritual once again. They knew how angry Pul will be if they failed.

Very little shaking took place below. The spirits stopped.

"How can this be?! Petra and the whole area is unstable... It is part of the great rift..." they told each other.

They turned to the rain. A spirit jolted out of formation. It screeched and then all of them reached out into the heaven. Booming thunder and huge lightning above them. Then they brought down their arms in fury towards Petra. Powerful rain slammed unto the city. Very quickly torrents began to fill the lower areas of Petra. But just before the waters started to threaten the people. Inside the bottom of the basin, the solid rock, split wide open and the earth itself swallowed the flood. No amount of rain caused it to flood. [87] The storm subsided and within moments, it stopped. But the day was unnaturally very dark. A very uncomfortable feeling over everyone.

The news crew breathe a sigh of relief. This was the first time that they had seen actual spiritual activity and warfare, and it's clear that they're on the right side of the battle. Now, they wonder what's next.

CHAPTER TWENTY-ONE

Thy Kingdom Come

Just east of Jerusalem, a great portal opened in the sky! A turnpike of marvelous spiritual activity! The angel turned to the news crew and told them that the same things that are happening over them are also in five other portals around the world. [88] Everyone below can only stare up to the heavens. awestruck.

Sean looking up asks, "What is it?"

The angel answered, "That's Jacob's ladder. All these portals will be used by God's Host. When the armies reach the surface of the earth, they will become Joel's army and fight from point to point. Jesus and his Bride will come first here to Petra... Edom. Then on to Jerusalem."

There were now great billows of fire unfolding around the opening in the sky. And lightning fired off continually around the host. This lightning was of all the colors of the rainbow, not at all natural. At the center of the host were a multitude of people on horseback wearing white robes, the Bride, with a single horseman leading them from the front.[89] The angels and the host (armies of God) began to pour through. They came down swiftly and with purpose, creating streaks of light trails flowing through the sky. Their bearing was from east to west and they appeared to be tracking directly to Petra.

The rest of the heavenly hosts which followed were angels, Seraphim, Cherubim, and Ophanim. There weren't just a few thousand angels, there appeared to be millions! They were spreading out in every direction and obviously had assignments to accomplish. The angels traveled like lightning from point to point. The skies were lit up with their presence, all of this had the earth lit up brighter than noon day. There was a deep rumble coming from deep in the earth.

When the heavenly army arrived at Petra, the horseman and host came down inside Petra from overhead! There was a period of silence for Pul's troops outside the entrance to Petra. They did not know whether to run or just hold their ground. Maybe this army was part of Pul's forces? They didn't know. Suddenly, the blockade at the entrance of Petra, the two story high concrete wall exploded from within and then dissipated into nothing. Not even smoke was left. The heavenly army blew through the opening like wind led by the Lord of the Host, the Elect One, Jesus!

Pul's troops began to fall backward at the Lord's presence. Then everyone outside Petra which had Pul's mark, the mark of the beast, were killed. God's angels were gathering the spirits of the slain as quickly as they could and leading them away. The heavenly army without hesitation turned north and proceeded towards Jerusalem, following the Lord of hosts [90]

Back in Jerusalem, Pul and his officers saw the heavenly display, knowing he had only moments to get to his stronghold. He scrambled down into his bunker, almost missing a step. Pul feared being killed by a sword. He went towards his table, still covered with his plans and maps. His face was wet and flushed. His hands trembled as he answered a call from one of his field generals.

"Sir, request to pull back! Sir! Please! Request to pull back! Please!" the field general begged.

Pul stammered, "S-s-stand... Your ground." Then Pul cut him short.

Pul's forces were in disarray. The general barked orders but was drowned out by the thunderous gallops of the horses.

A young Assyrian soldier, one of thousands, froze in fear where he was. He tried to hold up a missile launcher towards the heavens. But, before he could even pull the trigger, a mighty heavenly warrior swung his sword swiftly through him, releasing the young man's spirit from his body.

The heavenly army attacked Lucifer's pitiful demons, and his angels were dropping in obeisance to God's Army. Lucifer's angels had actually lost their battle to Michael (the archangel) and his angels several days earlier in heaven.

Pul lost more composure by the minute, mumbling to himself and attempting to control his tremors.

Marodeen approached and act concerned, "Pul! Oh, my god, you look pale! I have to check your blood pressure."

"Can't you see? I don't have time for this!" Pul said.

"Please let me help you. The last thing we need right now is for you to have a stroke!" Marodeen insisted.

As Marodeen leaned over Pul, he drew out a ten-inched dagger from inside his sleeve and plunged it into Pul's chest. [91]

Pul flinched as if pricked slightly by a small needle. Until his face contorted. Marodeen got up and revealed Pul clutching his chest. Pul looked up at Marodeen in shock, who had laid Pul on the floor face up.

Marodeen spoke with regret, "Pul you've become an animal. A beast. And when animals go rogue, we put them down. I'm so sorry."

"Marodeen?" Pul whispered.

Pul briefly looked up from the floor and saw Father Ibrahim attacked by several of Pul's generals. Pul's eyes flickered, slowly losing their focus. Father Ibrahim's lifeless body was now on the floor. Pul convulsed. Then suddenly a host of demons jumped out from his mouth like frogs abandoning their host. Complete darkness.[92]

Pul felt himself being lifted up. He opened his eyes once more. He looked down. This time, he saw his own body in a pool of blood. He looked to see who could be holding him up. He was startled to find two of the biggest and strongest angels he's ever seen, hoisting him by his arms. He tried to struggle from their grasp but they took Pul straight up thru solid rock and out of the bunker. They emerged into the air outside and just outside the temple complex. Pul gasped as he looked out on the city. All of the structures which had been built by men had become rubble and the people were gone. Only the temple mount and the temple remained. The Mount of Olives had been cleaved in two and the Lord of Host, JESUS, was standing at the temple. This time, he had not come on a colt. This time, he has conquered. [93]

The angels took Pul into the wilderness about fifty miles north east of Jerusalem to a location called Dudael. Flying in the spirit, they approached the Al Safa lava flow. Pul's breathing quickened and he yelped as they swiftly dived towards the center and through the jet black basalt surface. They descended into the earth. After a moment, they slowed to a stop. They were in a vertical shaft disappearing down. There was no light at all except that which radiated from the angels. The angelic escorts placed Pul in chains. There were now four more angels who went down below Pul, while another four angels hovered right around him.

The angels down below him were sounding horns and shouting, "Arise and see Pul Bet Sharruken, the man who destroyed the world, who was worshiped as a god!" [94]

Pul was then lowered down to their level. They stopped. Then he saw them. The spirits of the dead came to the edge of the pit to see Pul. They were grouped by their nations and by families in compartments inside the walls. Their compartments were completely without light but Pul can still see their faces, contorted and angry beyond belief.

The dead shouted, "Is this the man that destroyed the world?! He's just a man... And just as weak as we are! Come, join us... Please, please, put him in our cell!"

Pul turned away. But there were more shouts and curses from the opposite side of the pit.

Then the angels presented Pul to another group in another cell and they travelled down further into the pit and repeated the process again and again. Each level down the spirits became more vehement than the last until every person in Hell had an opportunity to see Pul in chains, and cursed him. Finally, the descent was over. Pul looked up at them. His face was devastated, darkness filled his face.

The angels spoke to Pul, "You will not have the pleasure to join your people in their compartment... Because you have destroyed them..."

They went further down and deep within the earth. Then, they hovered above a large magma lake. Pul screamed and cried as they slowly approached it. He writhed against his chains. Pul turned to see Father Ibrahim in chains being put in the magma right behind him. Then the angels pushed him into the lake. His bloodcurdling screams echoed never ending.

CHAPTER TWENTY-TWO

Any Question?
Yes Millions

When the Lord stopped in Petra before he blew open the blockade and destroyed the armies outside. Jesus entered Petra on his white horse. The angels and his bride began to sing their praise to him.

"Holy, Holy, Holy... Behold the Lamb of God who removed the sins of the world by his blood. Behold his kingdom has come."

The news crew gathered to see Him. They looked up to Him in awe.

Laura attempted to touch the muzzle of one of the huge and mighty horses of the bride. She flinched a little as its breath touched her skin. She touched its gleaming armor and hair. She returned her attention to the Lord who patted his horse's neck very gently. She saw Him leaned forward and whispered in its ear. Every muscle in the horse's body flexed and tightened. Then, suddenly the horse turned and made its way to Petra's exit, through the winding canyon.

A loud and bright explosion. The Bride and angels flowed out of Petra behind the Lord. The battle was on!

Meanwhile, some of the saints from heaven gave their aid to the people who packed and prepared for their return to Jerusalem. The Jews sorted themselves out by tribes. The heavenly saints came to them to give each tribe their banner,

Juda, Reuben, Gad, Asher, Nepthalim, Manasses, Simeon, Levi, Issachar, Zabulon, Joseph, and Benjamin.

As the bright light disappeared, some of the angels remained with the people in Petra, preparing for their departure. The angel who had helped the news crew approached them.

"Do you have any questions?" asked the angel.

The news crew in unison answered, "Yes, Millions."

The Angel turned and beckoned for a young man to approach them. The young man came over. He had a white robe on.

"He is from the bride of Christ." He said.

"Well, we can't thank you enough!" Gus spoke. He reached out to shake his hand.

Isaac shook his hand as well. "It's a pleasure to meet you, Mr... I'm sorry. I didn't get your name"

The man replied, "Oh, it was Thomas Taylor."

The crew suddenly fell silent.

"Did you say Thomas...Taylor?" Sally asked in shock.

He nodded.

"It's the same name as the Oklahoma prophesy man." Isaac said.

"It can't be him. We know for a fact that he'd be pushing seventy years old." Laura said unbelievingly.

"I know it's a silly question but... might you be his son?" Evelyn asked.

Thomas replied, "No, I never had a son."

The crew's mouths were all agape. Isaac barked with laughter.

"This is our Tom! He changed just like the scripture said he would!" Isaac exclaimed.

Laura gave Thomas a hug. She cupped his face in her hands to admire it.

"Yes, Thomas is in his prime again... Only better. He will never age. Death is swallowed up in victory!" said the angel. [95]

Thomas said, "I'm grateful that you were able to use my collection of data. It had taken me decades to put it together."

"We could not have succeeded if it hadn't been for you, Tom." Sean added.

"You're too kind but I had only assembled the data with the Holy Spirit's help.

The truth all came from God's word. By the way, Sean, is that my pen in your pocket?" He continued, "Keep it, I have a new name now."

The angel walked away. The crew and Tom turned to see where he was heading.

He turned to them.

"It's time to go home... to Jerusalem. We all have work to do." Said the angel

They all started walking towards Jerusalem.

THE END.

REFERENCE LIST

[1] A map of Ermia Iran and area. See page 135.

[2] Introduction to Shah of Iran. See page 136.

[3] Dur Sharrukin drawing. See page 137.

[4] Eagle faced Seraphim photo. See page 137.

[5] Scripture refer. Hebrews 11:10 A foundation whose builder and maker is God.

[6] Scripture refer. Isaiah 19:23 A road from Egypt to Assyria.

[7] Scripture refer. Daniel 7:20 His look more stout than his fellows.

[8] Photo of Roman centurion helmet and eagle head Seraphim. See page 138.

[9] Photo of Ophanim. Scripture refer. Ezekiel 1:15-21 See page 138.

[10] Scripture refer. Daniel 11:21 Flatteries.

[11] Photo of Asshur and Assyrian tree of life. See page 139.

[12] Iranian parliament seating plan, to show minorities. See page 140.

[13] Scripture refer. Sampson, Judges 16:29-30.

[14] Scripture refer. Isaiah 17:1 Damascus, taken away from being a city.

[15] Scripture refer. Jeremiah 49:1-2 Amman, it shall be a ruinous heap.

[16] Scripture refer. Jeremiah 49:35 Elam (Iran) I will break the bow of Elam.

[17] Scripture refer. Zephaniah 2:1-4 Woe to the inhabitants of the sea coast.

[18] Scripture refer. Revelation 8:8-11 A mountain (asteroid) burning with fire from heaven. And a star falling (comet) called wormwood.

[19] Map of Nineveh (Modern) the ruins within Mosul. See page 141.

[20] Map of Mosul, not used

[21] Scripture refer. Revelation 17:12 Ten commanders, ten kings which have no kingdom.

[22] Scripture refer Revelation 17:16-17 The beast with the ten.

[23] Scripture refer Daniel 7:8 The little horn, from the ten.

[24] Scripture refer Daniel 8:8-11 A fourth horn and beast into Middle East.

[25] Scripture refer. Revelation 11:1-2 Measure the temple, and them which worship there.

[26] Scripture refer. Revelation 11:2 Outer court given to Gentiles.

[27] Scripture refer. Daniel 11:27 And they shall speak lies at one table.

[28] Scripture refer. Luke 17:35-36 One shall be taken and the other left.

[29] Scripture refer. I Corinthians 15:51 Behold, I shew you a mystery.

[30] Photo of woman and eagle, from statuary hall Capitol building. Page 142.

[31] Photos of Washington DC pediments. Page 142.

[32] Photos of Apotheosis of Washington in Rotunda of Capitol. Page 143.

[33] Scripture refer. Jeremiah 50:9 Assembly of great nations, (10 horns) Jeremiah 51:27 Ararat, Minni, Ashchenaz. (Turkey, Iran, Russia).

[34] Scripture refer. Ezekiel 29:10-11 Egypt desolate for 40 years from Syene to Ethiopia.

[35] Scripture refer. Ezekiel 29:9 The River (channel) is ours.

[36] Scripture refer. Daniel 11:40 The king of the East (Egypt) shall push at him (fourth Persian king).

[37] Scripture refer. Daniel 11:28 he shall return with great riches.

[38] Scripture refer. Daniel 11:28 his heart is against the holy covenant.

[39] Scripture refer. Daniel 11:29 he shall return and come towards the south.

[40] Scripture refer. Daniel 11:30 The ships of Chittim come against him.

[41] Scripture refer. Revelation 17:17 Agree to give their kingdom to the beast to destroy the woman.

[42] Scripture refer. Daniel 11:30 Have intelligence with them that forsake the Holy Covenant.

[43] Scripture refer. Jeremiah 51:27 Ashchenaz and nations from the north (Russia).

[44] A map of northern Israel showing, The valley of Jezreel. See page 143.

[45] Scripture refer. Revelation 16:16 And he gathered them into a place called in the Hebrew tongue Armageddon.

[46] Scripture refer. Ezekiel 39:9 They shall burn them (weapons) with fire for seven years.

[47] [47]. Scripture refer. Isaiah 28:18 Your covenant with death shall be dis-annulled.

[48] Scripture refer. Daniel 9:24 Seventy weeks are determined upon thy people.

[49] Scripture refer. Daniel 11:40-44 Sequence of events.

[50] Scripture refer. Daniel 11: 45 He plants his palace in the glorious holy mountain.

[51] Scripture refer. Daniel 11:38 In his estate he honors the God of forces.

[52] Scripture refer. Isaiah 10:29 He takes up lodging at Jeba.

[53] Scripture refer. Isaiah 10:32 He shall shake his hand against the mount... the hill of Jerusalem.

[54] Scripture refer. Revelation 11:3 My two witnesses.

[55] Scripture refer. Revelation 11:5-6 They have power to shut heaven.

[56] Scripture refer. Revelation 11:11 After three and one half days the Spirit of life entered into them, and they stood upon their feet.

[57] Scripture refer. Jeremiah 30:7 Even the time of Jacob's trouble.

[58] Scripture refer. Matthew 24:21 Then shall be great tribulation.

[59] Scripture refer. Revelation 7:4 There were sealed one hundred and forty four thousand of all the tribes of Israel.

[60] Scripture refer. Luke 21:21 Let them who be in Judea flee to the mountains.

[61] Scripture refer. Isaiah 14:31 thou whole Palestina art dissolved.

[62] Scripture refer. Daniel 11:31 Pollute the sanctuary of strength.

[63] Scripture refer. Revelation 11:11 After three and one half days the Spirit of life entered into them, and they stood upon their feet.

[64] Scripture refer. Revelation 13:15 As many as would not worship the beast should be killed.

[65] Scripture refer. Revelation 11:8 Spiritually called Sodom and Egypt.

[66] Scripture refer. Revelation 13:18 The number of a man (666).

[67] Scripture refer. Revelation 13:15 The image of the beast should speak.

[68] Scripture refer. Matthew 24:15 the abomination of desolation in the temple.

[69] Scripture refer. Daniel 11:37-38 He will not regard any god, he shall magnify himself above all.

[70] Scripture refer. Isaiah 14:11-13 How art thou fallen O Lucifer, son of the morning.

[71] Scripture refer. Revelation 12:9 He was cast out of the heaven and his angels were cast out with him.

[72] Scripture refer. Revelation 19:19 The beast and the kings of the earth gathered together to make war.

[73] Scripture refer. Revelation 16:12 the kings of the east.

[74] Scripture refer. Daniel 7:8 Three of the first ten horns plucked up by the roots.

[75] Scripture refer Revelation 16:12 dry up the Euphrates River for the kings of the east.

[76] Scripture refer. Isaiah 31:9 He shall pass over to his strong hold for fear.

[77] Scripture refer. Revelation 16:2 Grievous sores upon them that had the mark of the beast, and upon them that worshiped his image.

[78] Scripture refer. Joel 2:1-11 Joel's army, the army of God.

[79] Scripture refer. Hebrews 13:2 entertained angels unawares.

[80] Scripture refer. Revelation 19:6-8 His wife hath made herself ready. A great multitude.

[81] Scripture refer. Revelation 19:15 Out of his mouth goeth a sharp sword. With it he should smite the nations.

[82] Scripture refer. Isaiah 14:9, 15, 18, 20. The sides of the pit.

[83] Scripture refer. Matthew 6:10 The Lord's Prayer. Thy kingdom come thy will be done in earth as it is in heaven.

[84] Scripture refer. I Corinthians 15:52 In a moment in the twinkling of an eye... we shall be changed.

[85] Scripture refer. Daniel 7:25 He shall think to change laws and times.

[86] Map of Zedekiah's grotto. Under the old city of Jerusalem. See page 144.

[87] Reference to historic floods in Petra, not used.

[88] Scripture refer. Genesis 28:12 Jacob's ladder, a turn pike of angelic travel.

[89] Scripture refer. Revelations 19:14 The armies that followed him from heaven upon white horses.

[90] Scripture refer. Isaiah 63:1 who is this that cometh from Edom... mighty to save... to Jerusalem.

[91] Scripture refer. Isaiah 31:8 Then shall the Assyrian fall by the sword, not of a mighty man, not of a mean man. In his strong hold.

[92] Scripture refer. Revelation 16:13 And I saw three unclean spirits like frogs come out of the mouth of the dragon and out of the mouth of the beast and out of the mouth of the false prophet.

[93] Scripture refer. Zechariah 14:4 And his feet shall stand that day upon the mount of olives, and the mount of olives shall cleave.

[94] Scripture refer. Ezekiel 28:8 Bring thee down to the pit, to die the death. Isaiah 14:15-20 Is this the man that made the earth to tremble.

[95] Scripture refer. I Corinthians 15:54 Death is swallowed up in victory.

[1] <u>ERMIA</u>

[2] Shah of Iran
Introduction

Mohamed Reza Pahlavi

He was born October 26, 1919 in Tehran, Persia and died July 27, 1980 in Cairo, Egypt. He reigned from 1941-1979 and died in exile after being deposed by the Islamic revolution in Iran. While he is considered a Shiite Moslem officially, he had a close affinity to his ancient Persian God and heritage and was also too close to the western nations. The Shiite clergy was not happy with his modernization of much of Iran's education and dress. During his reign, he developed Iran into and empire with the help of oil money. He was highly criticized because of the extreme opulence of his government and the sharp difference from the general public.

[3] <u>Dur Sharrukin</u>

[4] <u>Eagle Faced Seraphim</u>

[8] Roman Helmet

[9] Ophanim

[11] Asshur and the Tree of Life

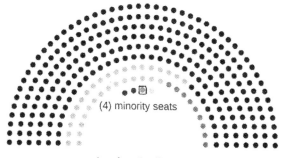

(4) minority seats

Iranian Parliament
Seating arrangement

[12] Iranian Parliament layout

[19] Nineveh and Mosul Map

[30] <u>Woman and Eagle</u>

[31] <u>Capitol Pediments</u>

[32] Apotheosis of Washington

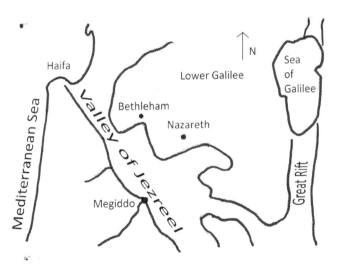

[44] Map of the Valley of Jezreel

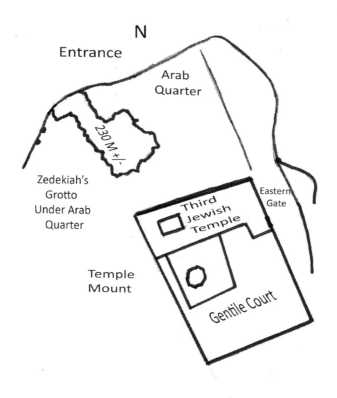

N

Entrance

Arab
Quarter

230 M +/-

Zedekiah's
Grotto
Under Arab
Quarter

Eastern
Gate

Third
Jewish
Temple

Temple
Mount

Gentile Court

[86] Zedekiah's Grotto

Printed in the United States
By Bookmasters